how to *Make* *a* *Wave*

how to **Make** *a* **Wave**

Lisa Hurst-Archer

Red Deer PRESS

Published by Red Deer Press
A Fitzhenry & Whiteside Company
1512, 1800–4 Street S.W.
Calgary, Alberta, Canada t2s 2s5
www.reddeerpress.com

Edited by Peter Carver
Cover and text design by Tanya Montini
Cover image ©2006 Courtney Milne. Photograph from
Courtney Milne's Pool of Possibilities Collection.7
Lyrics of " Moon River " copyright Johnny Mercer 1960
Image of eyes ©iStockphoto.com/najin
Thanks to Tegan and Sara for use of lyrics to "Missing You",
courtesy of Naked in a Snowsuit Publishing.
Printed and bound in Canada by Friesens for Red Deer Press

Financial support provided by the Canada Council, and the
Government of Canada through the Book Publishing Industry
Development Program (BPIDP).

Canada Council
for the Arts

Conseil des Arts
du Canada

Library and Archives Canada Cataloguing in Publication
Hurst-Archer, Lisa
How to make a wave / Lisa Hurst-Archer.
ISBN 978-0-88995-395-6
I. Title.
PS8615.U76H69 2008   jC813'.6   C2008-900064-1

United States Cataloguing-in-Publication Data
Hurst-Archer, Lisa.
How to make a wave / Lisa Hurst-Archer.
[240] p. : cm.

ISBN: 9780889953956
1. Families — Fiction. 2. Relationships — Fiction. I. Title.
[Fic] dc22 PZ7.H8778Ho 2008

For Evelyn,
Noah,
Keith,
Justin,
Caitlin,
Ben,
Will,
Isaiah

Thank you to Peter Carver
who believed in this book
from the beginning
and provided gentle nudges
along the way.

Thank you also to Morella
and Radhika for valued comments.

Chapter
One

Delia reads sad stories, listens to sad songs. She presses the repeat button to soak up every melancholy note, to see how far through the track she gets before the soppy lyrics and minor tones weigh down on her chest. Songs that tighten her throat as though she's swallowed whole fruit are delicious. Stories that tug on her and coax sadness from her belly, over her ribs, and up the ladder of her spine, fill empty spaces where any hope of ever seeing her mother again, of ever feeling normal, used to exist.

She lies on her stomach, gropes her hand down the wall next to her bed, and feels around on the carpet. Her fingers find an old photo, a crumpled candy bar wrapper, a single sock, a broken pencil, a paperback book that's been read and relegated to the discard pile. She yanks the book by its cover and rolls over on the narrow mattress.

Holding the book at arm's length, she scans the back jacket, and flips through the pages, tucking in the old photo as a bookmark. The picture is wrinkled and faded but it's stamped in Delia's mind in pure, clear color—there she is snuggled between her mom and dad, her smooth cheeks lifting her whole face into a smile. There she is—before the accident. Sometimes, Delia thinks she's stumbled upon a memory of the accident; she's not sure if it's a memory, the memory of a dream, or the memory of something she's made up. She's clear about one thing: the accident altered her life as though color and movement and sound had drained from a technicolor movie, leaving only silent, stilted shadows on a screen.

Oh, yeah, I remember this book. Even though it's been lying in the dark space beneath her bed for a couple of years, and she's already used it for a report she submitted a long time ago, she decides it will suffice for the homework that's due tomorrow.

She closes her eyes and mentally runs through the

plot. She doesn't cry when she thinks through the story-line; she's read the book so many times it has no effect—though she still doesn't get why the protagonist had to die. Wouldn't it have been better if she had survived her struggle and grown into a fairly well-adjusted individual, marked by her experience in a way that made her interesting and unique?

Delia has a habit of re-casting stories, of inserting persons she encounters into imaginary plots, of perceiving her own life as if it were a movie and she an actor waiting for direction from someone who knows how the script unfolds. Sometimes she envisions herself as the intended recipient or even the author of soul-wrenching lyrics she hears on the radio and down-loads onto her iPod to listen to again.

Delia rifles through her binder to find the book report form and flips through pages to extract the necessary information to complete it. It takes her eight minutes to finish, not counting the ten minutes it takes to find a pen. She tucks the report in her binder pocket, pulls off her clothes, and slips into one of her dad's big old T-shirts. She scrolls through her playlist, adjusts the ear buds, turns out the lamp, and sets the third track to repeat. Rolling on her side to face the wall, she pulls the covers to her chin and listens to pick up all the lyrics. The song cycles continuously, sifting words into her sleep—*screeching tires, busting glass, people all around, rain pouring down*—not unlike lullaby fragments that fell from her mother's lips and into her dreams when she was a small girl.

Delia sleeps as though floating on gritty bits of sand, vaguely aware that the ear-bud wires of her music player are tangled in her hair, that the sheet is twisted around her body, that ripples of music and lyrics skip and tumble around in her brain.

When daylight penetrates the curtains and seeps beneath her eyelids, Delia cajoles herself awake with a languid stretch, rises reluctantly, and makes her way down the hall to the kitchen. Occasionally, her dad is sitting at the table reading the newspaper, having arrived home from his night shift before she heads out to school. She's never told him that she likes to find him there—filling up the place in the empty chair. Instead, she grumps at him, complaining about the breakfast he's fixed or griping that he didn't wake her when she slept through the alarm. Delia doesn't know exactly why she feels so miserable, but she has a long list of possibilities. In lucid moments, she realizes that none of her reasons is justification to be cranky to her dad but—oh well—he's the main character opposite hers in the play called her life; that's his role now—to be the recipient of her misery.

Delia leans on the kitchen counter, waiting for her toast to pop. When it seems she's been waiting too long, she plops onto a chair, scrunches her knees to her neck, yanks her dad's shirt down over her legs, and draws her arms inside the sleeve holes. Her whole body is surrounded by the faded green *I Love Alberta* T-shirt. She hears the toaster pop but doesn't move from the comfort of the shirt/tent. If Delia doesn't get up to do a quick re-set of the toaster, she's not going to have time for a shower. She unfolds her limbs from their warm nest, steps her bare feet onto the cold floor, presses the toaster lever with her thumb — just enough to re-warm the bread — then flicks the lever, grabs the slices, spreads them with jam, and pulls off the crusts to eat the soft middles.

Delia is a master of the one-minute shower; as soon as she steps in, she lathers her skin, then shampoos while the soap is rinsing from her body. She's read in one of her dad's books, *Living More With Less*, that committing to the one-minute shower is a way to conserve water and do your daily bit for the environment. She wonders how many buckets of water she's saved over the past number of years, as bubbles slip from her wet skin and disappear down the drain. She uses an old bottle of spray-on conditioner that she found in the cupboard under the bathroom sink. It works pretty well and saves time. She combs her hair into a tight braid and slides on a little gel to keep the wispy bits from sticking out. She pulls on jeans and a hoodie, grabs her backpack, and stuffs two apples and a handful of cheese slices into the outside pocket. Delia is out the door by 8:17 so she'll just make the 8:25 bell.

Chapter Two

Delia is filling out a form that says she can go on a field trip with the eighth grade classes to the Calgary Science Center. She fills out the forms herself, forges her dad's signature even—the teachers probably know, though they've not made a big deal about it so far. Half the time she explains that she will bring the form in the next day, and then no one asks for it again.

Delia Oriana Greenwood. How could her mother not have noticed that the initials of her only daughter's name are D.O.G.? Delia never reveals her middle name to anyone (possibly, she told her friend Brittany, once). Whenever she's had to fill out a form at school, she writes in the appropriate space: no middle name. She thinks this is not quite a lie since it is no middle name a person would want if the names on either side of it create the initials D.O.G.

Delia doesn't know the middle name of anyone other than Brittany Anderson whose middle name is Rachel. She remembers when they were five years old, playing hospital in the living room, their mothers drinking coffee and planning some sort of function, probably a fundraiser for their kindergarten; Brittany insisted they make hospital bracelets with their full names on them, stating whether they were a girl or a boy. Delia noticed Brittany's initials and pointed them out—B.R.A. Brittany made her promise that she wouldn't tell anyone. She never has. Once you know something like that about a person, though, it's hard not to think about it every time you see her face. Delia sees Brittany from a distance in the school hallway; she wonders whether anyone else knows Brittany's middle name. It could be worse, she thinks; her mom could have named her Bethany Ursula or Hailey Ann or Pamela Irena Greenwood.

Delia writes no middle name on the appropriate line. She decides that if anyone knew her initials, she'd be called "Dogface" or they'd bark at her or some stupid thing. She's not handing out ammunition. She knows that a nickname has the power to stick. She'd acquired a nasty one back in third grade and thought she could shake it by winning the class spelling competition, but that feat seemed only to exaggerate the problem. Two weeks later, when she was crowned recess arm-wrestling champion, the nickname was dropped. Only one boy, Jamal Abaas, didn't step up to the challenge; he said it would be too embarrassing to be beaten by a girl. The ritual arm wrestles she had with her dad to determine who'd get to cook supper (he won, so he got to cook) finally gave her some payback. It occurs to her that this was probably her dad's intention all along.

Delia sits at the back of the class in the row farthest from the door, where there's no one sitting next to her on one side and no one behind. She likes sitting by the window. When she was in elementary school, she'd sometimes see her dad walking home from work after his breakfast of eggs and fried potatoes at a little diner around the corner. He wore his gray All Right Security uniform and a pale blue shirt. Delia would have to restrain herself, fight the urge to jump from her seat and open the window to holler out when she saw him. She used to feel proud to see him walk by in his uniform and shiny black shoes. Now she would feel embarrassed and hope that no one else in the class would see him swinging his arms and strutting long strides.

"Delia, can you please share with the class whatever it is that has captured your attention? I'm sure the whole class is interested in hearing."

A surging blush to her cheeks feels unbearably hot and she mutters softly, "I'm just filling out a form."

"We're discussing the prose piece on page twelve; you'll have to put that away... let's see this form... "

Mrs. Arbuckle strolls as though there's a string section playing in her head; she waltzes along the aisle toward Delia and stops at her desk. She stares down at the form that Delia has just completed. "Oh... uh... sorry, this is for science class. I'll put it away."

Mrs. Arbuckle snatches the paper, a look of small

triumph on her face.

"See me after class, Ms. Greenwood," she sings over her shoulder, emphasis on the *Ms.*, as she sways back down the aisle to the front of the room.

After class, Delia hovers by the blackboard, which isn't black at all. She stares at the rows and rows of stiff white letters slanting at precisely the same angle on the green board. She realizes that Mrs. Arbuckle must have written all this stuff during class, and it's obvious to Delia that she hadn't been paying attention.

"Ms. Greenwood, are you sure you are not forging your father's signature on school forms?" Mrs. Arbuckle stares down over the rim of her thick glasses.

"Uuh... I'm sure," Delia mumbles.

"Sure of what?"

"Uuh... I'm not sure."

"Are you trying to be smart with me?"

"No, Mrs. Arbuckle, I wouldn't try to act smart... I just didn't understand the question."

"I hope you understand that it's serious business

passing off someone's signature as your own. It's a habit that won't serve you well in your life, so you might as well stop now. Understood?"

"Yes, ma'am."

"Now, what about your book report?"

Delia shuffles through her binder to find the report.

"Here it is." She hands the paper to Mrs. Arbuckle and notices that her language arts teacher is trying her best to look stern and empathetic at the same time. It seems a bit try-hard.

"Thank you."

"No problem."

"I see it's not typed—you used a red pen, Delia. How am I supposed to mark it?"

"I'm sure you'll figure out a way."

Mrs. Arbuckle's stiff mass of copper-colored hair and pale powdery skin quiver as she removes her black-rimmed glasses.

"I'm sure I will, Ms. Greenwood."

Delia is jostled in a streaming throng of jean-clad
students along hallways lined with rows of metal
lockers painted the color of liver pâté. Her stomach feels
queasy. Her legs are like wood. She must move her legs
forward with careful intention; otherwise, she'll be floated
along like a log in the water and get stuck like a log in a
jam, unable to move. She moves robotically, not looking at
anyone, careful to avoid brushing against another person's
elbow, shoulder, hip. She detaches her body from the moving mass of seventh, eighth, and ninth grade students. She
heaves her forearms on the heavy steel-clad exit doors and
finds herself out back of the music room. From a single
open window—that must have been overlooked by the
security-bar installers—she hears a tuba sputter a long,
low growl as if it's coming from a big, old, slow-moving
creature. A clarinet responds with a squawk, sounding
like one of those brightly colored rain forest birds.

Delia drops to the asphalt, her backpack propped
behind her for a cushion, her arms wrapped around her
bent knees. Above a cacophony of toots and squeaks, she

hears a tapping of wood on metal and knows that Mr. Cadman is rapping his baton on his music stand, clearing his throat, bobbing his shaggy eyebrows up and down. Delia is having second thoughts about her decision to drop band class after only a couple of sessions with Mr. Cadman. She considers that she may have been able to bypass him and enjoy the music, enjoy learning to play the clarinet. She's always wanted to play an instrument and maybe write lyrics to her own songs. Perhaps it's not too late to get signed back into the class, but then she'd have to go to the vice-principal's office and get a form signed, etc., etc., etc.

She leans back and closes her eyes. A few moments of silence send a signal through the open window and she can almost hear the collective first breath of the senior band musicians. They're murdering "Moon River." Delia discerns Mr. Cadman's guttural eruptions gaining intensity until his harrumphing grows louder even than the trumpets. The music sputters into disjointed silence. Then the warbling flutes repeat a line until Mr. Cadman is satisfied. The band gasps its collective breath once again, and this time "Moon River" is taken up with a mellow vigor, sounding more like a river flowing along in the month of May, and not like you're in a muddy swamp up to your knees. Delia used to know all the words to "Moon River." Her mother used to sing it:

> *Moon River, wider than a mile,*
> *I'm crossing you in style some day.*
> *Oh, dream maker, you heartbreaker,*
> *wherever you're going I'm going your way.*
> *Two drifters off to see the world...*

Delia wonders whether it's a good example of irony (which she's studying in language arts class) that she had loved her mother to sing "Moon River," and it turned out that her mother was the old heartbreaker, gone off into the world, drifted away...

The bell rings—it's not really a bell, it's a disgusting buzzing drone—and Delia gets up, slings her backpack over her shoulder, brushes bits of gravel off her pants, and walks around the building to the side entrance. She slips into the art room with a few other stragglers. So far, the art teacher, Ms. Murti, seems okay. She hasn't done the power-trip thing yet and she doesn't make you gag with a sickeningly sweet voice. Ms. Murti's voice is soft and clear like a bamboo flute. She doesn't just talk about art, she gets so absorbed in painting and drawing that, twice already, students had to point out it was time to finish up. The other thing is she lets you choose your medium. So far this term, students have gotten to choose a color and work with that color in whichever medium they like: pastels, acrylics, watercolor, chalk.

Delia has a hard time deciding on either black or blue—eventually she chooses blue watercolor. She puts a thick paper sheet in a sink full of water and presses down her hands to hold it under as if she's drowning a cat or something. She doesn't like the sensation of holding the paper under the water; the paper feels like a living thing in her hands—she would never drown a cat. Delia is relieved when her fingers sense the sheet has absorbed water and become slightly heavier. She yanks the paper as if she's performing some kind of lifeguard maneuver and holds it on an angle over the sink to let excess moisture drip from the edges. Now she lays the paper flat on a board and begins to drip cerulean blue beads from her brush as though she's carefully administering a measured dose of medicine. A thin layer of water floats on the paper's surface. Delia's drops of blue paint billow and swirl like a living nebula, sending out puffs of cloud. The bell / buzzer drones to signal the end of class. Students stream out of the room and flood into the hallways. Delia and Ms. Murti are the only people who remain.

"Delia, you'll have to finish up now. I've got a lunch meeting. You can come in tomorrow after school if you like."

"I'm almost finished." Delia's words hang in the space between her fixed gaze and the universe forming on the paper in front of her—a blue world, a wonderful world, where she'd like to go, where she wouldn't care what other people think of her, how she looks; maybe her mother is there—away beyond the blue.

She takes off her painting smock—a faded old shirt from her dad's uniform—and heads to the sink to clean out the water jar and paint brushes. Delia watches the murky blue from her jar swirl and mix with the water from the faucet and whirl down the drain.

She likes art class. She likes Ms. Murti. She likes blue.

Chapter Three

The one good thing about her dad's working the graveyard shift is that he's home when Delia arrives after school, and he's usually in a good mood at that time of day. Delia hates going to bed knowing that he'll leave around 10:30 and be gone all night. Mrs. Pezesky, their next-door neighbor, used to come over and sit in the living room until Delia drifted off to sleep. Mrs. Pezesky stayed up to watch the late-night movie anyhow, so it was no inconvenience. At the start of the new school year, Delia assured her dad that it was no longer necessary for Mrs. Pezesky to come.

"Are you sure, Delia?"

"Dad, I'm almost thirteen. I hope I can take care of myself."

In the evenings, when her dad has gone off to work,

Delia watches movies, listens to music, or reads, though she's quit buying magazines—they make her feel uglier than she already feels. Sometimes she talks on the phone with her Aunt Shirley. Once she phoned when she heard a strange noise in the house, but Aunt Shirley must have been at work, so Delia called next door. Then she pretended that she was sorry, it was an accident, she had dialed the wrong number. She was too embarrassed to ask Mrs. Pezesky to come over and sit with her, though she desperately wanted to.

"I'll keep an eye out just the same," said Mrs. Pezesky. "You call me if you need to."

One of the crummy things about her dad's working this shift is that he makes the supper—though they've long since stopped arm wrestling for the privilege—and she does the dishes. He likes this arrangement. He has stacks of yellow-paged cookbooks with titles such as *Diet for a Small Planet* and *The Enchanted Broccoli Forest.* Too bad he just doesn't get that Delia hates beans. He's proud that he makes his beans from scratch—they don't come from a can. He soaks beans in the fridge overnight and puts them on to simmer when he gets home from work in the morning. When he wakes up in the late afternoon, he whips up some concoction with the beans and makes up a name for it such as "baked beans à la apples" or "spicy bean delight."

"Uu-uugh! Daa-aad! Please. Not again."

He laughs and doesn't take her seriously, and she eats the beans anyway because she knows he tries so hard.

Once, he made cake from a mix and he didn't know how to make icing, so he slathered on whatever was handy (Delia's version of the story). He improvised a recipe because he didn't have the right ingredients and made something better (his version). Now, their favorite dessert—Delia has to admit it's true—is "golden yummy cake": yellow cake from a mix, apricot jam spread between the layers, a heap of whipped cream on top.

This evening they're having macaroni and cheese and, as usual, he puts in onions and big chunks of tomatoes so that Delia will eat some kind of vegetable.

Afterwards he fries two bananas, sliced lengthwise, with a bit of brown sugar and butter, a dash of cinnamon and orange juice. This is another of her dad's favorites. Delia appreciates his efforts, though she thinks that he worries, fusses too much over her. He should go out in the evenings once in a while—have a beer, play shinny hockey, or something. When Delia was little, he used to play hockey a couple of nights a week—"the jelly-belly league," he'd grin.

Delia has a memory of being in a cold arena, huddled beneath blankets with her mom on wooden bench seats, sipping hot chocolate, and cheering each time her dad carried the puck. It's a scene from the period of her life that's imbued with vibrant, crystal color—she's red-cheeked in the icy arena air—or it could be the thrill of watching her dad or the warmth of burrowing into her mom's shoulder that colors her lips and cheeks like candied apples. A few photos of her dad in a hockey uniform—before the accident—are stuffed in the back shelf of the living room closet, but he hasn't laced up his skates in years.

There are no photos of the accident, and Delia is not quite sure whether the black and white film she plays in her mind is something she's made up or dreamed.

If the sky is thick and cool, the color of gunmetal, and if she makes her eyelids heavy so she's peering through slits of light, or if she's sitting in the back seat of a car and the windows are fogging up and it smells like damp wool and the radio is crackling—then she sees it all clearly. What she remembers is sitting in the back seat, her eyes following a water droplet trickling down the window glass. She sees through the wet film on the window where the water bead dripped to create a clear streak; outside, the sky like heavy steel blotted with wet snow, streetlights, headlights, storefront lights shining and blinking, though it isn't nighttime yet. She feels the effort of the car's tires churning in slush. She sees, in the front seat, the outline shape of her mom's head—the damp air creating a halo of frizz around her—the curve of her mom's back as she bends to fiddle with the radio dial, Uncle Billy reaching to roll down the window to flick out his cigarette butt.

A dull thud from behind makes Delia's spine heavy, makes the car slice through snow and careen into traffic. Shards of sound: shattering glass, crumpling metal, footsteps in snow, strange voices—grown-up voices that sound like children crying—each sound clear and brittle, falling in slow motion like the water drop on the window glass.

Delia had whiplash, a broken rib, a bit of bruising, a shattered cheekbone, a seriously long and deep laceration on her face—nothing life-threatening. Her neck was sore and stiff; her back ached; her face felt puffy and numb and strange. She was taken in a wheelchair for x-rays, rolled along on gleaming floors past doors half-opened onto shadowy rooms.

It wasn't all bad in the hospital. People came to visit. They brought stuffed toys and cans of ginger ale. Aunt Shirley brought a bubble-bath and powder-puff set in a pink box. She sat next to Delia's bed whenever she wasn't at work. She painted Delia's toenails and combed her hair. She read *Charlotte's Web* and made the voices of all the different animals. Sometimes Aunt Shirley stopped reading and cried and blew her nose. This made Delia uneasy. It was as if she, Delia, had been chosen for the seat of honor next to the birthday girl who was opening a present; it turned out the present was one that the birthday girl didn't want anyone to see, but from where she sat, Delia couldn't help but notice. This was the first time Delia had seen a grown-up cry. She tried not to stare.

A man with a vase of flowers popped his head into her room and said, "Delia Greenwood?" He handed her a tiny envelope, which he'd detached from a plastic stick. Delia opened it. The card said *Get Well Soon*. It was from their neighbor, Mrs. Pezesky. The man put the bouquet of pink and blue carnations on the window ledge.

Delia liked the big bed that could be adjusted to different positions. Aunt Shirley turned the handle at the foot of the bed and plumped up the pillows so Delia could sit up and look at the flowers from Mrs. Pezesky, and the treetops and the birds flying by on the other side of the big window.

Delia's mother was in the same hospital, on a different floor. It was strange for Delia to think that her mom was somewhere in the hospital—she could have been in the room above her or directly below—in a room with a bed like hers, with people, their hair in nets, carrying food on trays, and nurses bringing pills in little paper cups and glasses of water with bendy straws, with a button to push in case you needed help, and faraway voices coming over the speakers. When Delia went to sleep at night, she thought about her mom in her bed somewhere in the hospital and wondered whether it was dark in her room too, and whether her mom was thinking of her too. Delia's mom had three broken ribs, a fractured leg, a shattered pelvis, internal bleeding. Aunt Shirley said it would take a while before she was back on her feet, but not to worry, she'd be good as new; she just wouldn't heal as quickly as Delia. Aunt Shirley said kids were resilient—they bounced back sooner.

Uncle Billy was in another hospital on the other side of the city, and people whispered that he was in a coma.

Delia wasn't sure how he got in the coma or what a coma was. When Delia asked, "What's a coma?" Aunt Shirley said, "Don't worry, he'll wake up soon."

On the day Delia left the hospital, her dad took her on the elevator to the fourth floor so she could visit her mom. She was surprised to see her mom lying flat and still on her back in a dimly lit room. There were no flowers, no teddy bears. A machine with dots of blinking light was suspended from the wall. A strange woman—Delia wondered who she was—lay in the bed on the far side of her mom's room. Her dad stood in the doorway, his hand pressing her shoulder, encouraging her to move toward the bed where her mother lay. Delia stepped closer to the bedside so she could hear her mother's shallow voice.

It sounded as though her mother had heavy wet sand in her mouth. "Delia. Sweetie. Let me see. You. They fixed you up. Pretty good didn't they? You get to go home today. Make sure you. Get the bandages changed. You and Daddy. Take good care of one another."

Delia's mom grabbed her hand and gave it a little squeeze. She closed her eyes and smiled weakly.

"Well. Bye then. Bye sweetie. See you soon."

Delia and her dad held hands but she could barely keep up with him; he was walking with great big giant steps. She was pulled down the green-walled corridor, past sweet-sick-minty-smelling rooms, past doors that said *NO ADMITTANCE*, past a woman wheeling a clear plastic bulge that dangled from a metal pole, the bulge connected to the woman's arm by a plastic tube.

Delia watched her father's finger jab at the elevator button just above the level of her eyebrows. She heard the ding as the elevator doors slid apart. She stepped sideways into a space that was big enough if she drew her shoulders forward and pulled her elbows together. The doors closed and Delia counted the drops: one… two… three. She fixed her gaze directly in front, staring at the white curly hairs on a man's freckled back. The man was slumped in a wheelchair, his blue hospital gown parted between the places where it was tied to reveal his speckled flesh. The elevator whooshed to a stop, the doors opened. People stepped quickly, carefully, through the space between the parted doors into a space where they could breathe bigger again.

Delia sucked her breath through rounded lips and made a big sigh.

She sat next to her dad on a plastic chair the color of an orange Popsicle. She swung her feet, clanging them on the metal chair legs, so that her dad had to tell her to stop it more than once before a taxi painted with black and yellow checkers appeared on the other side of the big, heavy, glass doors. Her dad swung her up in his arms and carried her to the taxi. The driver opened the door for them and put her bag with her slippers and pajamas and teddy bears in the trunk. Her dad placed her on the seat and buckled her seatbelt, even though she knew how to do up her own seatbelt. Delia pressed her bandaged face to the window as cars–houses–shops–trees–people streamed by. She hadn't been at ground level for more than two weeks. It was a whole new world.

Chapter Four

What really bugged Delia was that her mom had said, "See you soon." She remembered that. Clearly: *see–you–soon*. She received each word, as if they were three links in a chain and she held on to them; she held them close. Delia didn't see her mom again until four months later, when Uncle Billy died. She hasn't seen her since.

Her mom's sister, Shirley, came to the house, though. She fussed over Delia and looked at her in a way that made her feel strange. She broke open Vitamin E capsules and rubbed the oil on her face as if she was rubbing something that was broken and her magic balm would put it back together again.

Her dad told her about Uncle Billy at the breakfast table one morning. She slurped cornflakes and tried to sound out the French words—*FLO-kon de MAY-is*—printed on the back. Her dad spoke dryly, matter-of-factly, over the rim of his coffee mug. "Uncle Billy passed away in the middle of the night. Peacefully. Slipped away… after all that trouble for everyone. So, I guess that's one good thing."

That night her dad went to the funeral parlor and her grandmother came to stay with her at the house. The phone rang while her grandmother knitted and watched TV in the other room. Delia whispered into the receiver and told her mom, "Yes, come over… no, Dad's not here."

Delia sat in the kitchen, staring at the microwave clock, which had been glowing a luminous green 12:02 for a number of years. She waited and listened for her mother's step at the back door. She made no sound as she reached to unbolt the lock. She moved aside and her mom was standing on the mat by the door, her hair glistening with tiny ice crystals, her cheeks damp and pink, her coat moist with the scent of winter night. She dropped to her knees and grabbed Delia, pressed Delia's face to her shoulder. Their two bodies rocked back and forth, back and forth—as if they were one body—as if an invisible hand was pushing them—a kindly hand, pushing them on a swing in the park on a Sunday afternoon. Her grandmother came into the room to put her cup and plate on the counter next to the sink. She didn't say anything at first. Then she said words in a flat line, "I see you're here."

Delia's mom said, "Yes, Helen, I'm here. Give me a few moments, please."

Her grandmother sighed, "You'll take what you want anyhow," as she turned and walked from the room.

Her mom placed her hands on Delia's shoulders and spoke close to her face so that Delia could smell her mother's breath like wet brown leaves and too-ripe strawberries. She watched her mother's lips move and the tip of her tongue touch the ridge of her teeth. She heard the words that formed when the lips moved. "No matter what anyone says—you are a beautiful, strong girl, Delia. You must believe that. You're strong and you're smart and I know you're going to be okay. I have to go, Delia. Okay? Okay, sweetie? I love you—you know that, don't you?"

Her mom left quietly through the back door. Delia went to her room. She didn't want to talk to her grandmother. A million thoughts were pressing her brain and Delia whispered them to the wall next to her bed: *Why is grandma mad at my mom… where did my mom go… if she loved me, she would stay… wouldn't she?*

A car's headlight beam swept into her room and tossed shadows through the flimsy curtain her mom had made from some material she'd used for a dress. There wasn't enough cloth left over to make anything else, so she had hemmed the edges and hung it with thumbtacks over Delia's window. Now Delia wished it was a proper curtain, thick enough to block out hurtling columns of light. The approach of another car made shadows shift and loom large on her wall. Her heart raced; she hoped it was her dad.

She was awakened in the morning by the urge to pee. She emerged from the bathroom to see her grandmother sitting in the swivel rocker next to the living room window. Her grandmother wore a blue tracksuit. Her orange-tinted hair was set with hot rollers. She sat facing the window; her back—straight as a board—blotted the morning light flooding the room.

"Grandma, where's my daddy?"

"He'll be home anytime now, I'm sure…"

"He didn't come home last night?"

"He'll be home soon—don't you worry, dear—he's taking care of things."

"What kind of things?"

"Don't worry your little head about grown-up things. Look here, Mrs. Pezesky made us a nice carrot cake. She's going to stay with you tomorrow when we go to the funeral."

Delia pranced to the kitchen. "Oh, yum… yummy," she chirped as she knelt on a chair, poking her finger into the cake and licking the sweet, creamy icing.

"What's a funeral? Is it scary?" Delia asked her grandmother, who had followed her into the room and now stood over the table, her hands on her hips.

"No. It's not scary..." Her grandma's voice was soft like the icing on Mrs. Pezesky's cake. "Sometimes it can be sad. People remember the person who's passed away and say prayers for them. Sometimes they cry because they realize how much they will miss the de... de-ceased."

"What's the deceased?"

"Well... you know, Delia, the person who passed away."

"What did they pass away?"

"The one who died, Delia, the person who died. Uncle Billy—he died."

"You mean he's dead like my Muffy?"

"Yes, Delia, he's dead like your Muffy, but not like your Muffy. When people die, it's not like when hamsters die. When people die... they go to heaven and... they're with God and they're not hurting anymore... they're all better." Delia's grandmother spoke the words as if she was choosing pieces of fruit at the grocery story, the pieces that had no bruises. She picked out the words, one at a time.

"Is my daddy going to die?"

"No, Delia, your dad is just fine... he'll be along soon. I'm sure he's going to live a good long life. Look at me—I'm no spring chicken—I've lived a lot of years."

"Are you going to die, Grandma?"

"Well, I'm not going anywhere right now. How about Mrs. Pezesky's carrot cake? Would you like a piece for breakfast?"

"Okay."

"How about some juice?" Her grandmother was already pouring apple juice from a carton. "Here you go, sweetie," she said as she placed a glass of juice and a piece of carrot cake onto a plastic-coated placemat that was shaped like a map of Canada.

Delia didn't like when her grandma called her "sweetie." Her mother was the only one who called her that.

"Thanks, Grandma," she mumbled and picked at the cake.

Chapter Five

Delia roots around on the back shelf of the living room closet; it's dark in here, so she rifles through the stack of shoeboxes with a flashlight. She finds the box she's looking for under a large yellow envelope. She carries the envelope and the box into the living room and sits cross-legged on the cold, bare floor with the contents of both strewn in front of her. She examines one of her dad's old hockey team photos. Delia focuses on the player with the big grin in the middle of the back row. She recognizes the face of a younger Uncle Billy, though it's from a time before she was born.

She puts the picture to one side and begins, now, to study a photo that she remembers having seen as a young child. It's a high school picture of her mom wearing a long, blue dress with a scooped neckline and one sparkly button. She has her hair swooped up, except for a single curling tendril that hangs on each side of her face. She is beautiful. She is happy. Her eyes shine. She looks as though this could possibly be the best moment of her life. Uncle Billy has his arm around her. He's not looking at the camera. He appears to be aware only of Delia's mom.

She turns over the photo, which has a crease like the vein of a leaf growing up the center. It looks like a leaf that's fallen to the ground, unnoticed by passers-by as it lies buried beneath a mound of yellowed leaves; a gust of wind scurries the mound and Delia walks by at that moment, picks up the leaf. She checks to see if there's a date stamped on the back. No date. Just a handwritten note: *Cheryl, I love you forever. Billy.*

Delia squeezes a scarlet bead onto an old china plate; pressing the metal tube between her thumb and forefinger, she coaxes a blood-red serpent onto the palette. She smears bloodandgutspulsingheartsmouldering-embermadashell-colouroflove onto the canvas. She applies layer on layer of

varying red shades—cerise, scarlet, crimson, vermilion—
with random, reckless strokes. And then, breathless, as if
she's run a race and collapsed at the finish line, she is
done. She's used gobs of paint to make a dense red blob
like throbbing scar tissue on the canvas. Delia cleans
her brush and palette and empties her water jar at the
sink. She sponges a smear of red from the floor. She
slips out of her painting smock, hangs it on a hook at
the back of the room, packs up her things, and props
her painting on an easel to dry. She walks out of art
class, though there's still another twenty minutes left
in the period. Delia's painting really does look like the
inflamed tissue that grows into a protective coating
over a wound.

A staccato voice whines over the loudspeakers, "The
following students are to report to the main office
at 3:20: blahblahblahDELIAGREENWOODblahblah."

Delia's palms are sweaty and it feels like there's a heavy
stone in the pit of her stomach. She stands in the waiting
area of the main office. "Can I help you?" A secretary

behind the counter smiles blandly as her fingers continue moving on a keyboard.

"Uhm… you called my name."

"What's your name?" she asks as her glazed eyes dart from her computer monitor to a clipboard of paper. *She's pretending she doesn't see my face*, Delia surmises.

"Delia Greenwood." Delia speaks casually, attempting to hide her nervousness.

"You're to make an appointment with Ms. Pearson, the guidance counselor. Her office is across the hall."

She walks across the hall and stands in front of the heavy wooden door that bears a black and gold name-plate: Ms. S. Pearson. *I wonder what her middle initial is*, thinks Delia. *I hope it's not A or O.*

Delia knocks on the door, even though it's open a crack.

"Come in," a voice speaks in a neutral tone.

"I'm Delia Greenwood. I'm supposed to make an appointment with you."

"Yes, Delia, come on in. Sit down. Let's see… you're

in 8D, is that right?"

"Uh-huh."

"Can you come see me at the beginning of second period tomorrow—Thursday?"

"I guess so."

"So, I'll see you tomorrow, Delia. We'll take the whole fifty minutes to talk. Okay?"

Delia loads the dishwasher while her father sips strong black coffee and reads the newspaper. They've just finished a supper of fried egg and tomato sandwiches and canned peaches for dessert.

This is one of Delia's preferred meals. There's not too much he can do to ruin it, although sometimes he cooks the eggs so they're scabby and brown around the edges.

"So, Dad, I was called down to the guidance counselor's office today." Delia speaks in a not-too-loud voice to test whether he's listening.

"Are you having a problem with something?"

"Not that I know of..."

"Are you doing all your homework and everything?"

"Sure I am. It's so pathetically boring and easy, I usually get most of it finished during class while the teacher is blathering on."

"Well, maybe you should listen better."

"Maybe you should too, Dad." Delia doesn't speak the words loud enough for him to hear; at least she doesn't think so. She's not sure whether he has called the school to suggest that Delia meet with a counselor.

Delia has quit peppering her dad with questions about her mom.

"Where is she? When is she coming back?" She had tugged and cajoled at every opportunity.

He'd replied in a voice as soft as a child's who waits, sure and clear-eyed, for Santa's reindeer to appear, "We'll wait and see."

Delia had kept at him with an avalanche of questions, until one day he said, "Quit pestering me. I don't know. You'll have to ask her."

That was enough to shut her up. It clearly was not possible for Delia to ask her mom anything—it had been years since they'd heard from her. References to her mother had become increasingly rare, like the occasional puddle of water that appears on their basement floor, the source of which remains a mystery. It was like that when the subject of her mom crept into a conversation—out of the blue—and then a scurrying to mop it up and pretend it never happened.

Ever since the funeral, Delia's dad tightens the place where his jawbones meet into a hard pulsing knot whenever anyone speaks of her mom or Uncle Billy. Delia knows not to speak of certain things by observing the juncture of his jawbones. She's not aware that she does this; it's as though she has the instinct of a horse that knows to avoid unstable ground. Speaking (or not speaking) about her mom and Billy is the barrier that exists between them—a barrier that is growing thicker and deeper like permafrost spreading its icy tentacles, chilling the earth so completely that it won't thaw in the middle of summer even.

Sure, Delia loves the quirky little things about her dad, his "expertise" in the kitchen, the way he calls out hello when either one of them comes into the house, even though she responds derisively: "Dad, you're not an undercover 7/11 employee, are you?"

She loves how he meticulously budgets their money and carefully counts out each paper bill when she needs clothes or "girl stuff," as he calls it. When he's finished, he slaps down another ten dollars and wags his finger to remind her not to spend it all in one place. He tells her always to have extra cash on hand in case she should need to take a cab or something. She's taken a cab just once—when she was little—so it's not as though she'll be hailing one anytime soon. She has stashed the extra cash in her top drawer, but she's not thinking of taking a cab, she's thinking of taking a plane somewhere, maybe out to Vancouver; maybe she'll visit her mom's sister, maybe next summer. Or when she's old enough, in a few years, she'll move out, move away from here. Little does her dad know that he's topping up her travel fund when he slips her an extra ten dollars.

Delia does appreciate his efforts though—how he spends hours at the library choosing books that he thinks they both might like, or how he whips up meals that he believes to be nutritious and tasty. She can feel him hovering over her, worrying and not knowing how to make a connection. There is so much that Delia loves about her dad and there is so much aching empty space between them.

Chapter Six

Delia hunkers in her room, flopped on her bed, listening to music, reading, grasping at flitting bits of memory as if she's swooping a net to catch butterflies; but she can't contain the butterflies, she only can watch as the memory bits flutter away and disappear.

The other day in art class, while she was making a collage of various yellow shades, she experienced a sensation, as though she were drawing a line around a memory, as though she were pulling a slipknot around a gopher and had nearly captured it.

She recalls that she had once visited a farm—some friend of Uncle Billy's—when she was a little girl. She doesn't remember anything about the house or the people who lived there or why she was there with Uncle Billy.

She retrieves scent—earth, sky, dry grass, dung—from the furrows of her memory now: Uncle Billy stomping across a field of long, flat grass that looked to Delia like the golden-yellow hair of an enormous woman. He hollered and cracked boulders to scare off a big black bull. Then he took Delia's hand and walked a long way off in the other direction, surprising her when he dropped to the ground then motioned for her to do so. They lay with their bellies on the earth, their chins lifted like cobras, waiting, watching for the furry little sentinel to pop its head from a burrow, chirp a signal, scurry, and disappear. A labyrinth of gopher tunnels connected the holes from which the creatures emerged, seemingly wary but too curious for their own good.

Uncle Billy fastened a piece of string with a slip-knot to one end of a stick. He lay a little distance from a hole, patiently grasping the stick, ready to yank it as soon as the creature emerged. Delia plunked low-bellied to the earth like a four-legged animal; from this rodent-eyed perspective, grasses and spent flower heads appeared as a jungle of overgrowth. She lay silent on the cold, hard ground, her eyes fixed on the slip-knotted end of string, the sun hot on the back of her head even while a cold pulse from the earth chilled her belly. Uncle Billy, the stick ready in his hand, grunted softly when he changed position to relieve his stiff knees. Delia knew he was doing this for her. He endured the discomfort, waited for the right moment to jerk the stick, draw the string, and capture the gopher in the loop end—all for her benefit.

She focused on the gopher mound, her arms and legs taut and aching with the effort to hold them still, waiting for a furry tuft to poke from the hole. She was ready to scream out, to warn the little creature to stay in the hole and avoid the waiting snare. When the pointed little face appeared—glistening eyes and flickering ears—she saw that it trembled. She held her breath, wanted to hold the moment—so close to this small creature that she could see its heart pumping wildly beneath its skin. She couldn't bear to frighten the tiny curious thing and so she couldn't call out a warning and save it from the gathering snare on the end of Uncle Billy's stick. Her voice was stuck some-where in her body and she couldn't find it.

When Uncle Billy presented her with the trembling creature as if it were a fun new toy, she faked a smile. She wanted him to think she was appreciative of his efforts even though it made her feel sick to see the tiny animal trapped and frightened. Delia was as much a bundle of nerves and confusion as the gopher. She always felt confused around Uncle Billy—uncertain as to how he fit into their family, where he belonged.

Delia works intently now on her collage, creating patchwork scraps of yellow hues. She rotates a piece of paper that she's colored yellow with oil pastel and slips it through her thumb and forefinger to tear a shape, a shape that, surprisingly, reminds her of the outline of her mother's lips, the asymmetrical shape of her mother's mouth.

Holding the paper mouth in her hand, Delia surveys a scene from her childhood as though it's been pressed in a heavy book of yellow-edged pages: there is her mom at the kitchen table, standing behind Delia's dad with a coffee pot at the ready. She tops up his cup and then—a flickering moment—she looks at Uncle Billy, who is at the far end of the table, facing her. Delia is sitting at the side of the table, with her dad at one end, Uncle Billy at the other. She's trying to follow their conversation, when she glimpses her mom and recognizes the look on her mother's face. It's the look she sometimes has when she sits at the foot of Delia's bed when she thinks Delia is asleep—it's a look of pure, unconditional love. Delia realizes that her mom's gaze is fixed on Uncle Billy. Her mother's lips are parted and she could be about to say something, but she doesn't.

Delia works at fitting memory pieces into some kind of recognizable shape. It's difficult to do when people are not exactly brimming with information. Delia collects bits and snippets of details and fits them together. It occurs to her, a few years after Uncle Billy has died, that he's not really her uncle—there is no blood relation.

Sometimes it feels as though she's forcing the pieces together, like the time she worked on a jigsaw puzzle over the Christmas holidays and eventually resorted to using scissors to make pieces fit.

Here's what she's figured out so far: Billy was her mom's high school sweetheart and he was her dad's linemate on the Junior A hockey team. He was the star player of the Calgary Canucks. Then he went off to play in Ontario and was drafted from there to the New York Rangers. Billy played three NHL games for the Rangers before a knee injury became so severe he was unable to skate. He drifted around the hockey world for a few years as a scout or a coach, and then no one heard from him for a long time, until one day he showed up at Dave and Cheryl's place in Calgary. Dave and Cheryl had been married the year Billy was drafted to the Rangers. He had sent a note that joked how he, Billy, had made the big time, but that Dave, his linemate back home, was the lucky one.

Delia is sick of her yellow collage. She likes yellow a lot better when it's mixed with red or blue. Something about yellow makes her queasy—yellow snot, puke, runny yellow egg yolks, Uncle Billy's yellow hair; that's the only way to describe it. His hair was yellow, not blond, or golden, or platinum. Yellow. So were the ends of his fingers—from all the cigarettes he smoked. If he was such a great hockey player, how could it be that he was a smoker too? It must be because his pro hockey career was washed up so soon. Delia thinks that must have been a disappointment for him. She knows how depressed she felt when she didn't make the volleyball team. *What the heck? Why am I so preoccupied with Billy? Who cares? He was an old friend of my parents, an old, washed-up hockey player that couldn't get a job and had nothing better to do than hang around our house.*

She is snapped back into the present by Ms. Murti's voice. "Class, it's time to put away your work and tidy up." It's a relief to put away the yellowish hodgepodge she's created—it looks to Delia like sad layers of forgotten pages and rotting leaves.

Delia is late for her appointment with Ms. Pearson, the guidance counselor. She wonders whether she has been singled out to appear for a consultation or whether all eighth grade students are scheduled for a guidance session. She sits and waits in the little outer room for Ms. Pearson to call her in.

"Delia, how's it going? Any concerns? I just want to let you know that it takes a while to adjust to a new school year, to develop new friendships; that's normal. You're aware of the many teams and clubs, the yearbook club, I assume? There are many opportunities for eighth graders; you just have to take initiative and get involved. There's a different expectation about personal responsi-blahblahblah. So, that's understood?" Ms. Pearson looks at Delia from across the desktop, which is clear and free of clutter.

"Uh-huh… sure." Delia's not quite certain what she has just agreed to.

"So, any questions?"

"No. I don't think so."

"Well, if you have anything you wish to discuss, please come and see me," Ms. Pearson looks directly at Delia—face to face. Her concern seems genuine.

"And, now, Delia, I'd like to talk to you about the consent forms that you've submitted. There appears to be some question about your father's signature."

Delia fesses up immediately. "You know, Ms. Pearson, it's just me and my dad. My mom took off years ago and he does the best he can, but he works all night as a night watchman, and he sleeps all day. I don't like to bother him much. So, if you don't think these field trips are safe, then I won't go. I know my dad would be really upset if anything happened to me. I was in a bad car accident once and I think that's enough. I'm all the family he's got."

"I'm not saying enhancement excursions are unsafe, Delia. I'm talking about replicating your father's signature. We all can't just forge signatures because it's convenient."

"Everyone is not forging signatures, Ms. Pearson. I think we're talking about me. If you'd like me to disturb my dad when he's trying to get a bit of sleep, I'll do that... it just doesn't seem fair." Delia is flabbergasted with herself. Why is she lying and carrying on like this? Why doesn't she just say: Sorry, I won't forge my dad's signature again? Instead, she's taking up the challenge as if it's a high and mighty principle of hers. She's enjoying the game, getting a bit of a kick by playing Ms. Pearson along. Really, she shouldn't be taking advantage of the fact that Ms. Pearson is a first-year teacher. But Delia is bored and she can't resist.

"So, Ms. Pearson, with your permission, I think the best course of action is to agree to allow me to participate in the field trips that are safe. If there is a danger to me, if the students are participating in unsafe activities, I think it's best that I not participate. I wouldn't want my dad to worry." Delia flashes a wide-eyed, brimming-on-the-edge-of-tears look that she's used before to milk sympathy from certain types of people—

people who feel sorry for her because of her face. She can spot them a mile away.

"Yes, Delia, that's a good idea. We'll leave it at that." Ms. Pearson speaks kindly, glancing at the clock, at the appointment schedule on her computer screen. "We'll talk again, of course. Be sure to book an appointment if you need to talk about anything—anything at all."

Delia stands up to leave Ms. Pearson's office. When she's halfway down the hall, Delia laughs out loud.

Chapter Seven

The buzzer drones its hideous tone and students pour out of classrooms into the hallways. Delia is not sure which class she has next. She goes to her locker to check her schedule. A group of girls is clustered in a circle nearby. They toss their heads and run their hands through their long, straight hair, slouch their tall bodies, pout their lips, and make their eyelids heavy when they're not all talking at once, as they do just now: *I'm going for a smoke. I have a French test. Who cares about French? Moi, my dad will kill me if I fail. Did you wear that yesterday? No. Yes, you did. Wait for me. Oh my god, there's Madame Fournier. I have to go; meet me in the washroom as soon as I'm finished the frickin' test. I'm going to Starbucks; I need to do my Social homework.*

Delia must consider whether it's a Day Three or a

Day Four, and what comes after second period in either instance. She stares at the floor in front of her locker as she tries to clear her mind. She concludes that it's a Day Three and that language arts class is next.

"I'm so glad my mother doesn't buy my clothes at Wal-Mart," one of the girls declares loudly as the group turns to face Delia, sweeping her over with a synchronized up and down glare. These words don't hurt her; they don't touch her. She knows how she dresses; she's comfortable with the clothes she wears. She dresses how she wants to. What hurts are the whispers she hears from behind as she walks away. "Oh my god, did you see her face? You guys, that was so mean. I didn't know she was a freakin' freak. I feel so bad... wouldn't you hate to have a mess like that on your face?"

Delia weaves quickly through the hallway, not making eye contact with anyone, pulling her shoulders and elbows close to her body, trying to make herself invisible. She slips into L.A. class, hoping not to be noticed.

Mrs. Arbuckle is at the blackboard writing notes for

today's lesson. She prefers traditional teaching methods, she says. What could be more boring than copying copious notes from the blackboard into exercise books? Delia considers the ridiculousness of this term; "exercise" is a word that's worthy of going along with "blackboard" (greenboard), "school bell" (hideous buzzer), "guidance counselor" (easily duped), and "girls" (b/witches).

Delia digs her pen out of her backpack so that she can begin "exercising." She writes furiously, paying no attention to the words that she copies until she comes to a passage that reads:

> *I have tried to present sympathetically the struggle of a boy to understand... the ultimate meaning of the cycle of life. To him are revealed in moments of fleeting vision the realities of birth, hunger, satiety, eternity, death. They are moments when an inquiring heart seeks finality, and the chain of darkness is broken.*

These are the author's words from the book her group is studying in L.A. class. Delia has not begun to read it yet. She knows that when she starts to read the book she'll likely not be able to put it down until she is finished. It's a Canadian author, W. O. Mitchell—W.O.M. is much better than D.O.G., Delia supposes. The book is called *Who Has Seen the Wind*. Delia especially likes the last line on the page of her exercise book—*an inquiring heart seeks finality, and the chain of darkness is broken.*

She likes the title too, and she gets to thinking whether she has seen the wind ever or whether she only has seen the effect of the wind—leaves fluttering, litter scuttling, flags flapping, waves rolling. It may be like the thoughts a person has; you can't see the thoughts inside a person's brain but you can see the effects of those thoughts. Delia might not be able to see other people's thoughts, but she can see the reverberations when they cast looks at her in the hallways.

She wonders what color she would use if she were to

paint people's thoughts, what colors she would choose if she were to paint the wind; could she actually paint wind, could she paint thoughts, or merely render the ripple of their effect? She is reminded of a verse from *The Big Book of Rhymes* that still sits on the shelf in her bedroom:

> *Who has seen the wind?*
> *Neither I nor you.*
> *But when the leaves hang trembling,*
> *The wind is passing through.*
> *Who has seen the wind?*
> *Neither you nor I.*
> *But when the trees bow down their heads,*
> *The wind is passing by.*

Delia loves the delicious rippling of the poem's breath on her skin—it will stay with her a while, like the dappled imprint you find on your arm or your face when you've been lying a long time in the grass. Some poems stay with her that way.

She will bring the novel-study book home and read in bed long after her father has gone off to work. She'll read until she falls asleep with the light on. Maybe she'll be awakened by a noise in the middle of the night; if so, she won't turn out the lamp. She'll arrange her blankets and old stuffed toys into a heap and then scrunch her body into a ball so that any intruder couldn't discern the shape of a person lying alone in the bed. She does this most nights.

Chapter Eight

Delia's birthday is this coming Friday. It's not something she looks forward to. She usually spends the day lying in bed and feeling crummy. She never attends school on her birthday, but probably no one notices. It's no big deal having a birthday, thinks Delia; everyone in the world has one—basically it means you haven't died yet. Delia detests the girls who make a fuss, adding and deleting names on party lists, depending on who they like on any given day. They talk loudly about crossing off this guy or that girl and matching up couples. And what's with birthday bumps, pinches, spanks, eruptions of singing, and springing surprises on people? It's enough to make her feel nauseous. Delia was sickened a few years ago when Betsy Daigle was asked whether she'd like a "milkshake" for her birthday—"milkshake: noun – group activity whereby boys lift and shake a person who wears a skirt above their heads, and drop said person to the ground when sufficiently shaken." When Betsy, sweaty and distressed, comes to class after recess, the teacher asks whether Betsy is okay, and Betsy replies that she's been running and has a cramp in her side. Delia knows the truth. She knows that Betsy has been given a milkshake for her birthday. She can't understand how Betsy can cover for those guys.

On Delia's sixth birthday, Uncle Billy stood in their living room in his leather-sleeved hockey jacket.

"Yup, dinner and a movie for my two best girls."

"What a nice surprise, Delia. Uncle Billy is taking us for a surprise for your birthday." Her mother's voice sounded cheery.

A few months earlier, Uncle Billy had arrived at their doorstep. Delia absorbed snippets of Uncle Billy's story as he sipped coffee and smoked cigarettes at their kitchen table. He and her father played cribbage and her dad said nothing, mostly, and Uncle Billy talked and talked and apologized when he accidentally cursed, saying he'd been in too many hockey locker rooms. Uncle Billy had been helping a hockey team in Buffalo but it just hadn't worked out.

"Buffalo is an awful place; it's no place a person wants to be; it's got that damp kind of cold that chills your bones," he said.

Delia pictured Uncle Billy on the edge of a frozen prairie, stamping his feet to keep the cold from creeping into his bones, hollering out to his hockey players while a herd of shaggy buffalo snorted and pawed the cold earth nearby. She'd seen a picture in a book once: hundreds of raging shaggy beasts and a tiny Indian man, dressed in a wolf skin hiding behind a rock, pointing his bow and arrow. Uncle Billy didn't have a wolf skin, only a hockey jacket; he had no bow and arrow, only a hockey stick. It was no wonder he didn't like Buffalo. Living in Calgary at Dave and Cheryl and Delia's house must have been a whole lot better.

Uncle Billy asked where she wanted to go for her birthday, and Delia said she didn't know. So what did she want to eat; Delia said French fries. They drove downtown to the Dairy Lane. Uncle Billy opened the door and bells tinkled above their heads. They sat on red leather stools up at the counter. Large white globes hung from the ceiling and cast pools of light on glass and chrome. A lady in a pale green dress, the color of meadow grass, wrote with a pencil on a thick pad when Delia told her what she wanted to eat. The lady brought French fries with ketchup in little paper cups, cheeseburgers with pickles, and milkshakes with tall, skinny spoons. They were the only people in the restaurant and Delia was aware that anyone passing by on the sidewalk could have looked through the big picture window and seen them, as if they were sitting inside a giant television screen. She noticed her own reflection in the wide front window and bent her head to catch a glimpse of her mother's smile, Uncle Billy's smile, her own smile, shining from the faces of those people in the glass who were them and who were not them but rather the people watching them. The three diners—a man, woman, and child—ate, talked, laughed. Anyone watching through the window would have thought they were a happy little family.

On the drive into downtown, against the flow of traffic, they had heard a voice on the radio warn of a blizzard, though it was just the middle of October. People were scurrying from their workplaces—eager to get home—not darting into shops or dawdling on street corners. The cars heading out of downtown sat bumper-to-bumper, puffing clouds from their tailpipes.

Inside the Dairy Lane, with her mom and Uncle Billy, Delia was warm and happy and full. The world on the other side of the window was far away—snowflakes dotting the cold gray sky like splotches on a cardboard backdrop—while the scene inside the little diner glowed.

The plan had been to walk over to the movie theater, but by the time they finished their meal and Uncle Billy finished his cigarette, the temperature outside had plummeted and snow blanketed the streets.

"I'll go warm up the car. You girls wait here."

Delia and her mom waited inside the restaurant while Uncle Billy fetched the car.

"Why didn't Daddy come for my birthday?"

"It's his hockey night, Delia, the first game of the season; he didn't want to miss it. He's really sorry… he'll have birthday cake with us later, after the movie. Uncle Billy is going to be back any minute now. He's going to take us to the movie theater. You want to see the Sleeping Beauty movie, don't you, sweetie?"

Delia was in the back seat, her mom and Uncle Billy in the front. The wiper blades whacked thick wet snow that splatted the windshield. Headlights and street lamps threw soft beams that looked as though they were coming from a faraway place through holes in a heavy curtain of sky. Delia's mom fiddled with the radio dial to pick up a weather report. Uncle Billy announced that he should get some new snow tires as he rolled down the window to flick his cigarette butt. A bead of water formed on the fogged-up window nearest Delia. Her eyes followed the water droplet's trickling descent, and Delia glimpsed the world on the other side of the glass through the clear path it traced on the steamy window. It felt to Delia as though there were two worlds; an inside world that was safe and warm and an outside world that was strange and cold. She felt the thud in her bones when the car was hit from behind and hurled into traffic. She felt her spine pressed into the space between two colliding planets.

Delia's dad is pleased that he's surprised her. He's hung balloons and a paper banner with letters that look as though they've been scrawled by a child's hand:

Happy 13th Birthday Delia,
From your Dad
xxxooo

He's managed to hide the cake—"a golden yummy cake" with apricot jam filling and a mountain of whipped cream—and now he carries it ceremoniously to Delia's room. One lighted candle stands crooked, its flame flickering as he warbles, "Happy birthday to you, happy birthday dear Delia, happy birthday to you." Delia props herself on her elbows, then flings her head back down on her pillow.

"Ughh... Dad. Why did you have to?"

The happy expression on his face wavers at the corners of his mouth. Delia doesn't mean to hurt his feelings.

"Dad, you shouldn't have."

"Quick, blow out the candle before it melts. Make a wish."

Delia extinguishes the flame with a puff of breath. Make a wish. There are a thousand things for which she could wish, but she's stopped making wishes, saying prayers, and imagining a better place somewhere over the rainbow where her mother might live.

"Thanks, Dad," she smiles.

"Shall I cut you a piece?"

"Not now... maybe later. I'm not feeling so hot."

"You're sick? What's wrong?"

"I'm okay—just a little tired, a bit of a stomach ache."

"Would you like tea? I can make you some tea."

"Only if I can have it in bed."

"I don't see why not. It's your birthday."

Delia spends the day in bed reading *Who Has Seen the Wind*. At first, it's boring—a slog to read—so old-fashioned. Because there's nothing else to do, she really gets into the book. In a little while, she likes the main character, a small boy named Brian. She likes how he goes around with no one paying him any attention and just figures things out for himself. He gets this feeling like a soft, yearning thrum in his heart and he wants to understand where it comes from. He watches the people around him, observes with a longing to know the truth about God and heaven, about people and life, how things are born and how they die. He aches with wanting to understand. He loves the terrible beauty of the wind on the prairie, the quivering limbs of a horse, the delicate licoriced wings of a dragonfly, and, more than anything else, the mysterious wide-eyed boy with hair the color of ripened wheat who wanders the prairie alone—somehow he and Brian share a silent ribbon of knowing. Delia wishes that she knew someone like Brian, someone with whom she could share an unspoken bond of understanding.

Delia knows she shouldn't read the whole thing because then she'll be bored in L.A. class—she's in the advanced novel study group as it is. The group will take weeks to wade through the book. Delia will get distracted, perhaps secretly read another novel or doodle in her agenda—Mrs. Arbuckle will notice and come swaying down the aisle at her, bobbing her head like one of those dogs you sometimes see in a car rear window, the head seemingly not attached to the neck, her hair reined in, shellacked with a heavy dose of spray, and quavering like the fake dog head.

Delia shouldn't read too many chapters and get too far ahead, but she's at home in bed on her birthday. Her dad will sleep until five o'clock, when he'll rise, shower, and shave before making supper. They might play a little cribbage or kick around a soccer ball. Maybe she'll walk over to the video store and grab a movie, a bottle of coke, a bag of Doritos.

It's her birthday, so Mrs. Pezesky will likely pay a visit and maybe stay to watch the movie when her dad goes off to be a security guard. Aunt Shirley called and said she can't come today; she'll bring a present tomorrow. Delia could care less about a present. Today Delia has turned thirteen, but she feels as if she may be six or sixteen.

Chapter Nine

Delia sits in Aunt Shirley's kitchen. Shirley is the middle sister in her mom's family: Cheryl, Shirley, Sheila. When Delia was a little girl, she had a secret longing to be part of the circle of sisters—*CherylShirleySheila*; she had wished that her name belonged with theirs. On the *Sesame Street* program, they sometimes played a game: one of these things is not like the other ones. Delia knew her name was not like the sisters' names. She wished she had been called Sheena or Shelly, a name that could hold hands with theirs and come rushing on a breath of wind. Now she thinks how childlike it was for her grandmother to choose these names—embarrassing really—another good reason for her to swipe and chisel away at the god statues that were once the adults in her life. At one time Delia had thought that adults were wise and all knowing; she couldn't wait to grow up. She's beginning to see that adults have insides that are not much different than a kid's; they're scared of making mistakes, of not being liked. She sees how they say and do stupid things, just like kids do.

"So why didn't my mother come back after the accident?" Delia chews at the inside of her lower lip, picks at a nagging hangnail on her left thumb, fidgets in her chair. She peppers Aunt Shirley with incessant questions.

Shirley hasn't yet applied her makeup; her skin is pale and dark circles sag beneath her eyes. Shirley doesn't have any kids; she lives alone in an apartment. She used to have a boyfriend but she doesn't really need a boyfriend, she says—she makes enough money waiting tables, especially with the fat tips from the oil patch guys, to decorate her place real nice. She has a leather couch, an entertainment center with a plasma television and surround sound. "Who needs a boyfriend?" she laughs and waves her hand around the living room.

Delia sometimes stays overnight and sleeps on the

pullout in the computer room. The two of them eat junk cereal straight out of the box or paint their nails hideous colors while they talk or watch movies. One time, they slathered their lips with finger paint and made a line of kiss marks as a border on Aunt Shirley's bathroom wall.

"I'm not sure why your mom left after the accident, Delia. Maybe she thought it was all her fault. She probably felt guilty for being with Billy."

"Guilty? Why would she feel guilty?"

"Well, I know your dad wasn't too thrilled to have Billy around."

"But... but I thought they were good friends."

"They used to be friends when they were younger. Billy went away and your mom and dad got married. They lost touch. When Billy came back, it just wasn't the same. Your mom and dad had been married six or seven years and they had you. Billy hadn't moved on; he was stuck in a dream. I think your dad wasn't too thrilled to have him around."

"But I remember he lived with us for a while," Delia interjects.

"Yes, he did. That's right. When he came back from the States he lived with Cheryl and Dave for a few months."

"I remember one time my dad and Billy were yelling; it was the only time I ever heard my dad swear. Most of the time they got along though—they played cards and talked and stuff."

"I don't know about that. I remember your dad being agitated when Billy was around."

"But my mom really liked him, didn't she?"

Aunt Shirley sips from her cup of herbal tea. "Do you want to know the truth, Delia?"

"Sure, I do... of course."

"Your mom and Billy were an item when they were younger. I think your mom never stopped loving Billy. It's not that she didn't love your dad; I'm pretty sure she loved him a lot. It's just that when Billy came back, it brought up old stuff."

"What kind of old stuff?"

"Your mom and Billy—everyone thought they'd get married—but… but… then Billy went away… something happened… the rest is history."

Delia sits cross-legged on her Aunt Shirley's high-backed chrome chair. She looks down at her thighs, knees, shins, and feet floating beneath her on the underside of the smoky glass tabletop. They look to her like somebody else's legs, somebody else's feet. She lifts a porcelain cup to her mouth, hesitates, and instead of drinking, forms words on her lips—words that many times had been almost-shaped only to become heavy black stones for her to swallow. Delia spits out the words now: "The something that happened is me, isn't it? I'm not stupid, you know. I can handle the truth. My mom got pregnant, didn't she?"

"Yes, Delia, it's true. It's nothing to be ashamed of. You were born—a little earlier than might have been expected—but your being born, that was a good thing, a very good thing."

Delia doesn't feel better having spoken the words.

She doesn't feel relief; rather she's surprised by the words that have slipped from her tongue. It's as though she were a blind person who suddenly becomes sighted and sees something as familiar as her own hand for the first time; there's shock in finding that something so near could be unrecognizable. The words that had swirled in the soft, round silence of Delia's mouth and slipped down her throat a thousand times had tumbled from her lips, leaving a hollow, laughable residue on her tongue.

Delia lets loose a loud sigh and gets up from her chair. She wanders into the living room and stands for a long time staring out the window. Then she flops down onto the couch and muffles a sob that swells and unleashes tears and snot and staccato breath. Aunt Shirley follows her into the living room, crouching down on the floor by the sofa to rub Delia's back. "It's okay, honey, it doesn't change anything… your dad loves you… I love you… let me get you a blanket."

Chapter Ten

Delia leaps out of bed and dashes to the bathroom. She's groggy as she yanks her hair into a ponytail. Why doesn't she have nice straight hair like her mom and Aunt Shirley? She pulls on jeans and a zippered sweatshirt. There's no time for breakfast so she stuffs a few granola bars and an orange into her backpack. She walk-runs down the sidewalk, her heavy backpack jostling between her shoulder blades. She slips into class unnoticed, timely enough to be considered punctual.

Today Delia paints with red and blue. She's intrigued by the deep shade of purple that's appearing on her palette. She paints a picture of a room in which everything is purple: a table, chair, and purple window frame in an empty white wall. On the other side of the window she paints a purple sky with a blank white disk for a sun.

Delia thinks how purple is the only color that she knows for certain her mother hates though she doesn't know which colors her mother likes, which colors she paints her nails, her hair color even.

Delia remembers throwing a fit in the Sears store when she was about five years old. She was shopping with her mom, buying an outfit for some special occasion, and her mom held up a crushed velvet skirt with a little matching vest.

"Do you want the blue or the brown—or what about green, Delia?"

"Purple. I want purple, Mommy."

Her mother responded tersely, "Purple is the one color I detest."

Delia was bewildered. She had never considered the possibility that a color has power to summon strong feelings.

If she did get an outfit that day, it was entirely forgettable.

Delia is in a panic to gather her things at the end of art class. She's late again. She ducks into the washroom on the way to language arts class. When she's finished in the cubicle, she finds that she's not the only person in the facility. She averts her eyes, not wanting to look at the mirrors.

Three girls lean over the sinks, plying on lip-gloss and eyeliner. She doesn't want to squeeze between them to wash her hands; she doesn't want to have to speak to them, but it's obvious they aren't moving. She hovers near the sinks and they halt their babbling talk as if it's too precious to let resonate on the cold stone floors and walls and fall onto Delia's ears. Delia could care less about their blathering conversation; she just wants to wash her hands. They stare at her and she feels compelled to say, "Excuse me." One of the girls, who has just finished applying a dark line at the corners of her eyes, makes a ceremony of moving out of the way. She grabs her makeup bag and slams it on the counter, further from the sink that Delia uses to wash her hands.

Delia rinses her hands quickly and wipes them on her jeans. "That's so disgusting," she hears over her shoulder as she hurries out of the claustrophobic ladies' room.

Mrs. Arbuckle stares over the top rim of her glasses when Delia enters the classroom, and resumes her lecture. "So… we were talking about the young Brian's perception of God. Can anyone tell me how young Brian perceives God?"

A hand shoots up. "He sees God in the blue color he makes on a piece of paper—then he makes different colors and there's God, like spiders, then this little man appears in a beam of light coming through the window."

"Okay, then, what else?"

"God's this little man that's about knee-high and he's wearing a little—what does it say—a little, blue gum-drop hat and white rubber boots and he's got a lamb under his arm. He's like real friendly and he introduces himself, like, 'Hi, I'm R.W. God. Nice to meet you. Did you want me to kick anyone's ass or anything?'"

A ripple of laughter floats in the air of Mrs. Arbuckle's eighth grade L.A. class. A couple of students whose bodies are too big for their desks have their legs sprawled and their backs slouched; even they are flipping through the book now.

"Later on, God becomes this mean dude, who's sort of behind Brian's head, like when the teacher is punishing him for lying, and he's holding his hands up at the front of the class, he feels God behind him, judging him, making him feel bad," a boy at the front of the class says.

"And sometimes God is the beautiful, aching mystery of creation—the wind on the prairie." A girl who has black painted fingernails and wears a long patchwork skirt speaks softly.

The students have been assigned to three groups, with each group reading a different novel. They are comparing passages from the three books about certain themes: God, nature, innocence, death. Most of the students get a kick out of Brian's God, especially when Brian sings that God is on a leaf, with yellow cufflinks on, and he can belch if he wants to. Brian insists that it was R.W. God, not Brian, who let loose with a belch. His father tells Brian that it's silly for him to fib and insist that he can see God, to insist that God rides a vacuum cleaner and tells stories. Brian is adamant—it's not silly—he does see R.W., he does talk to him. Brian's father responds, "Let's just forget about this God business; let's just say your prayers."

The discussion for the rest of the class is about people's different concepts of God/Spirit and how one cannot prove or disprove another's spiritual experience. Soon they're talking about religious tolerance/multiculturalism. They go off on a tangent about whether a person is born with a concept of God / Spirit or whether they acquire it through exposure to other people's ideas.

Delia considers that a person's perceptions not only may be different than another person's, they may be different than they were last month, or yesterday even. She considers that her perception of Mrs. Arbuckle may have changed; it's possible that Mrs. Arbuckle may not be so bad—even though she is such a try-hard; it's possible that she may be like a kid, hungry to understand and to be understood.

Chapter Eleven

Delia walks home from school alone. She has what she needs in her backpack so she ducks out the side doors at dismissal time without having to go to her locker. She cuts across the school field, slips down an alleyway, and crosses the busy road that parallels the river at the crosswalk. A few geese loiter on a grassy stretch, waiting for bread crust handouts that some one is sure to provide. She skirts around the portly birds to seek a narrow footpath down to the river's edge. She steps her way through red-stemmed dogwood and scraggly *willow*.

She bends to pick up a flat smooth stone, a perfect skimmer. Her dad can make any stone skip—this one he'd likely zip along the water for thirteen or fourteen hops, thinks Delia. The first summer following the accident, the first summer her mom hadn't come back, Delia and her dad spent a lot of time on the river. They'd put in a little rubber dinghy and float along the clear, rippling water over speckled river stones. She felt safe in the dinghy, surrounded by a cushion of inflated rubber, drifting calmly beneath tall cottonwoods, watching cliff swallows swoop and dip. Sometimes she'd see beavers glide alongside their craft, slipping below the surface to emerge a long way ahead. Delia glimpsed the white tails of fleeting deer among the brush, and once she saw the curious face of a coyote slinking along the bank, watching them.

The next summer her dad bought a canoe. They drove southeast of the city with the canoe on top of the car, then unloaded it and stowed it in the long grass at McKinnon's Flats, driving another fifteen kilometers to drop off their vehicle. They hitched a ride back with a woman who lived in the area and ferried paddlers, for a few dollars, to their put-in spots. Delia didn't like the wobbly canoe. She constantly feared they'd ram into a rock and tip over. She was much more aware of the river's powerful tug than she had been in the floating dinghy. In the canoe, she was never sure whether to paddle left or right, whether to pry or pull. She didn't know that her dad did the bulk of controlling at the stern end of the canoe. He could manage the task of paddling on his own. He'd say things like, "Just sit back and relax." But she couldn't, she couldn't recapture the feeling of tranquility she'd had in the wide-bottomed rubber dinghy. Her fingers curled tightly around the neck of the paddle as she jockeyed to keep balance.

"Delia... look." Her dad's voice was soft with wonder as he pointed. Two giant white birds bobbed in the river, their long yellow bills positioned downward, ready to scoop wriggling fish.

"Pelicans, they're pelicans," he whispered.

The birds arched their backs and spread their wings to reveal a ribbon of black on their fanned feathers, and then—seemingly miraculously—their huge bodies lifted in the air, their wings stretched wide, and they were carried aloft. It looked to Delia as if it was their act of surrender, their trust in the currents that carried them into the air, above the river, and out of sight.

The memory of the pair of giant birds—as they lifted off, their wings outstretched, latching onto invisible air—comes to Delia now. In summer, she is always on the lookout for pelicans. One time she spotted a lone bird along the section of the river that runs near her neighborhood. Today, there's no chance of seeing a pelican—they've already begun their seasonal migration—but Delia scans the river up and down along the banks anyway. She's the only person along this stretch of river on this cool, gray afternoon. It's a good afternoon to feel lonely, to wonder whether you're even wanted, to wonder who your real father is.

Delia paces the living room with the phone tucked under her chin. She flicks through the remote to find *Oprah* or maybe a rerun of *Friends*.

"Hello, Shirley here."

"Aunt Shirley, I was just about to hang up. Do you know where my dad is?"

"No, honey, I don't... everything okay?"

"I was just wondering where he was... he didn't leave a note or anything."

"I wouldn't worry about it. He probably just ran out to the store or something. Call me back if he's not home in half an hour? Okay?"

"Okay. Aunt Shirley? I think I know." Delia sits down on the couch, her hands sweaty, her mouth dry like Styrofoam.

"Know what, Delia?"

"About my mom and Billy."

"What about them?"

"About how Billy is my dad."

"Who told you that? Did someone tell you that?"

"I just figured it out."

"But, Delia, Dave—your dad—is your dad. You know that."

"Yeah, I know that. I just have to let somebody know that I know the truth. It doesn't make any difference to me, really it doesn't. I just have to tell someone."

"Oh, sweetie, are you all right? Do you want me to come over? We could go to Tim's for coffee—you don't drink coffee, do you?"

"No, it's okay... okay, maybe you should."

Delia slams the door behind her as Aunt Shirley pulls up in her flower-painted Austin Mini. Ordinarily, it's pretty cool pulling up to stop lights and pretending to be oblivious to people's stares (people staring at the car, not her face), but today Delia's mind is preoccupied. She'd like to ask her Aunt Shirley a million questions. For starters: *Why didn't anyone tell me?*

"I didn't even get to go to my real father's funeral. How rude is that?"

"Whoa, hold on. Let me concentrate on the driving. We'll talk over coffee—tea or something."

Aunt Shirley is always trying to kick her caffeine habit and switching to either herbal tea or hot water with a lemon slice. Delia likes her better when she's back on caffeine; she's more like herself.

They stand at the counter waiting to grab the

attention of the woman who's wiping away smudges on the glass counter. Delia is accustomed to people fumbling for the right way to look at her—not gawking, not pity, normal; the same way they'd look at anyone. She and Aunt Shirley stand and stare at the racks of doughnuts: maple, chocolate, vanilla, sugar, cinnamon, sprinkles. They order two small coffees, double cream, no sugar. This is the first time Delia has had coffee without sugar but she doesn't let on.

They carry their cups to a little table with chairs that are fixed permanently to the floor. They sit, each one positioned an equal distance from the table. The arrangement makes Delia feel as if she can talk to Shirley as an equal partner at the table. It makes her feel grown-up to be sitting here in the evening, drinking coffee with no sugar and her dad not knowing where she is. She always feels like herself when she's with Aunt Shirley—the self she used to be before she acquired a facial disfigurement—as unselfconscious as any thirteen-year-old girl. Aunt Shirley doesn't seem to notice the thick scar that pulls at the corner of Delia's mouth and crawls in a curve, puckering the skin up to her eye socket.

"As I was saying, don't you think it sucks that nobody told me—that I didn't even get to go to my real father's funeral?"

"Delia, Dave is your real father; he's the one who raised you. The fact that your mom was pregnant when she married Dave—that didn't make a difference to him. Dave knew; he wanted to marry Cheryl. What I don't know is whether Billy ever knew—I don't think he did. I think Cheryl wanted Billy to go off and pursue his hockey dreams. When Billy left, Dave just stepped up to the plate. I think he knew what he was getting into. And she felt she was doing the best thing by providing a good family situation for her child, for you. She loved him too—don't get me wrong—it just wasn't the same as it was with Billy."

"Oh, my God, someone's finally actually speaking the truth to me."

"Delia, when were we supposed to tell you? I don't see how it makes a difference. Dave is your father. He loves you completely. You were six years old when Billy died. And your mom was in pretty rough shape."

"Where is my mom, that's what I'd like to know... do you have some secret information about that too?"

"I wish I knew. I miss her too. Sometimes I wonder if she's still—you know..."

"Alive?"

"Yes. I wonder whether she's still alive. It's been so long now."

"When's the last time you heard from her?"

"She sent a card once, from India. It was just a tiny square of paper with really small handwriting."

"She sent you a card? Do you have it? Can I see it?"

"I have it somewhere. I'd have to look for it. Listen, Delia—"

"What did it say?"

"She said that she was trying to put things right. That she was living in an ashram. That's all."

"So, basically, what you're saying is that she ran away from her life to become a religious fanatic in India."

"Yes, something like that. Delia, listen: it's not about you—it's about her. I guess that's what she thought she had to do."

"You're right about that. It's not about me, it never was. It was all about her. And Billy. He ruined every-thing when he came to our house."

"Really? Everything?"

"Not everything. My dad is so, you know, he's so good to me. I know he loves me. I've got some pretty good things going, for sure. But it's like I was cheated out of my mom. Why the heck were we in Billy's car anyway?"

"Because of you... because of your birthday. Billy wanted to take you somewhere special."

"Some birthday present—I wish I could give it back. But I can't, I can't give it back, can I?"

If it was possible to have a wish, Delia would wish that it was her sixth birthday. She would wish that she could say, no, no thank you. It's awfully nice of you, Uncle Billy, but no thanks. I'm going to have a pork chop and mashed potatoes with my mommy and daddy and afterwards we're going to sit on the couch and watch *The Brady Bunch*. Mommy and I will make popcorn and melt real butter on the stove. Daddy will go down to the basement, bring up two cans of Coke, and pour them into three glasses.

Delia feels a sudden pang; she should call her dad.

"Aunt Shirley, can I use your cell?"

"Sure, honey. Just punch in the number and press send."

"I know how it works… Dad?"

"Delia, where are you?"

"I'm with Aunt Shirley. We're having coffee."

"Coffee?"

"We're at Tim Hortons."

"Did you have supper?"

"No. You weren't home. I didn't know if you wanted to eat later or something. Where were you?"

"I had an appointment; I guess it ran late."

"What kind of appointment?"

"We'll talk about it later. Does Shirley want to come over for a bite to eat?"

Delia holds her hand over the speaker and leans across the table toward her aunt. "My dad wants to know if you want to come for supper."

"Sure. I can't stay too late though."

"Okay. We'll be there soon... about twenty minutes. See you."

Chapter Twelve

Sagarika—Hindu name translated as *wave; born of the ocean*

Cheryl is nobody's wife, mother, lover, daughter, sister, friend, companion, devotee. Cheryl is Sagarika—or perhaps the ghost of Sagarika. This is the only connection. Sagarika rises early in the morning. She kneels, lifts her cotton shawl from the sleeping cot made of woven string, and wraps the cloth around her shoulders. She lights the thin darts of kindling that have been arranged in the clay stove the previous evening. Already, a smoky veil drifts through the village where Sagarika lives in a mud and straw hut behind a cluster of other small huts. This was once the home of the grandmother of the family for which she does cleaning and washing. Sagarika was made to understand that the grandmother was stricken by terrible illness after her careless tending to a vat of cooking oil erupted into a fiery ball, causing the death of her husband and youngest child. The woman was able to get through the door and drop to the ground, rolling to smother the flames that scorched her sari but did not harm her. The woman lived a long and tortured life, alone in the hut, estranged from the rest of the family. No one in the family, or in the village even, will set foot in the hut. They believe it is cursed.

There is one room in the small earthen-floored dwelling. A neat bundle of cloth is tucked beneath an upside-down wooden crate near the far wall. A few items—a pencil, a thin sheaf of brown paper, a knife, a skein of white thread, a needle, a small piece of broken mirror—are arranged neatly on top. On another wooden crate retrieved from a garbage heap are glass spice bottles, a clay container of cooking oil, aluminum canisters of rice, lentils, and chickpea flour, a rusty-lidded jar three-quarters full of nuts. Beneath the crate, which has only three sides, are a brass pot and a clay bowl. On the wall near the door is a large basket in which sits a metal pail and a fat, round wooden stick. Above it, on a piece of rough board laid across the corner walls, is an altar upon which bronze figures of the deities, Shiva and Kali, dance among flowers, seeds, bones, beads, bells, a bowl of water, a smooth black stone; all is strewn on a swath of silk that shimmers in the early morning light.

Sagarika lights candles and incense in brass holders and the altar appears to cast a glowing essence, like some living thing, like the glistening coat of a wild animal prowling at dawn through rustling flora. Sagarika rests on her knees, her hands placed together in the *atman mudra*. She waits.

Perhaps she will hear it today. She listens, as she does every day, every moment of every day, for the faint, sonorous vibration that will gather and move like particles impelling ocean waves; she waits for the soft, sibilant song that will move upon the waters held within her body's skin. She heard it once; months of careful listening had yielded a soft thrumming song in return for her longing. She heard the song and answered the call; she became a particle and was taken into a rushing wave that gathered her together and dropped her on the shore of a new life in India. Almost seven years later, she is prepared to hear it again. She will not force the occasion; she will wait another seven years, another twenty years, if necessary. She is certain that she has created the capacity to hear—within her body, a tiny cup of listening is poised.

Meditative calm quickens the mantra that begins as an impulse deep within her belly and swims from her throat, "OM HARI OM." She rises, pours water from the altar bowl into her right hand, and sprinkles it upon the image of Shiva and his consort Kali. She places two grains of rice, which have been colored with kumkum and turmeric, as an offering to the god and goddess. She bows deeply before the altar.

Sagarika eats dal and rice, which she scoops with chapatti in her right hand from a wooden bowl. She boils a little water in a pot and sprinkles leaves for tea. Yogurt ferments in a jar at the back of the stove. She will have that this evening when she comes home from the washing.

Sagarika's hair is long and dark and oily. She looks like any of the women in the village, until you get closer and see that her eyes are a dark hazel, not brown. You notice that she wears no ornamentation—no tika or bindi on her forehead; no choorie bangles jangling on her wrists.

The skin on the palms of her hands and the bottoms of her feet is not quite so calloused and thick. Her complexion is not burnished buttery spice; it's more olive in tone. Her spine is a little straighter, more flexible since she has not always known the drudgery of work. She does not wear the mark of physical burdens upon her body. Her face carries the stigma of burden—sad lines at the corners of her mouth, a hollow point in the center of her searching eyes.

Sagarika walks through the village, steadying the large basket on her head with one hand as she moves. Inside the basket is a lightweight aluminum pot. Inside the pot is a wooden beating stick. She goes from house to house offering to do washing for a small wage. At one time it would have been unthinkable for a woman such as herself to do another woman's washing, but now many people make the pre-dawn trek into the cities to work in factories, data entry depots, and callcenters; they are not fussy about who does their household chores.

When the basket is stuffed full with soiled cloths and garments, Sagarika wraps a length of woven material over one shoulder and extends it around the back of her sari; she tucks in a slab of soap wrapped in plastic. Sagarika steps lightly, her head erect, along the path that leads to the water. Already, other women crouch over their washing pails, scrubbing reams of cloth and items of clothing at the riverbank.

People bathe in the polluted river, believing it has healing qualities, seemingly oblivious to the dark sludge that floats like menacing tentacles. A man hunches before a washing pail as he shaves with a straight razor and a mirror propped up on a rock. He smiles widely at his reflection. Another man sits in a lotus position as he plays a flute. Two boys wash an elephant while other children play and splash nearby. They have no fear of the great beast. One boy straddles the elephant's back while the other goads the animal with an *ankus*, cajoling it to turn and kneel.

Sagarika walks past a huddle of washing women, regarding them shyly with a *pranam* gesture. Solitarily, she goes about her work. She sets the basket on the ground, retrieves items one at a time, and beats them with the short, round stick to remove caked dirt and dust. When she has finished this pre-washing task, she fills the large pail with water from the river and hauls it up on the bank. She dunks cloth pieces in the pail of water, pokes the fabric with the end of the stick to get it thoroughly wetted, rubs the cloth on the slab of lye soap, and pounds and stirs it. She crouches over the pail, carefully tending to each item, and when this procedure is finished, she dumps the water and watches it trickle back to its source. She billows the laundry items in the river water to rinse and then spreads the clean linen and cotton on propped sticks to dry.

Sagarika came to India believing she'd been summoned by the call of her spiritual teacher, her guru, whom she had not met in the living flesh, but who she was certain existed in some transcendent realm. She journeyed to an ashram where each morning she performed *puja*, offering prayers and ritual washing. At the ashram she learned to chant and meditate; she prepared food, washed, and scrubbed.

One day she wandered away, ambling from village to village among throngs of people, jumbles of animals, carts, bicycles. She sat on the *ghats* where people gathered near the rivers, hoping for their sins to be washed away, burning incense, ringing bells, offering flowers, chanting prayers.

She wandered aimlessly and did not remain in any place long, until the night she laid eyes upon the Diwali lights, shining like stars spilled from the sky. Row upon row of *diyas*—little earthen lanterns—twinkled along the riverbank, lighting the river's dark path. She sat on sandstone rocks at the river's edge, observing the celebration of the festival of light, the New Year. She listened to the sweet, low drone of chanting, ecstatic shouts of "Sri Ram! Jai Ram!" and the rattlebangpop of crackers. She turned her face upward to bursting lights and showering fountains of fire from the sky.

Long after the people—brilliantly adorned and cleansed with sandalwood paste—return to their scrubbed clean homes and feast on sweet delicacies; after the celebrations and fireworks cease and they remember the marigolds and mango leaves laid upon altars in hope of a visitation by Lakshmi, goddess of prosperity and abundance—the river flows darkly.

Sagarika sits by the black river and listens for the thrumming song. She has no preconception of how or when it will come. She trusts that she will recognize it— she heard it once, clearly, long ago when she had lived far across the ocean, far across time, and lay in a hospital bed. In the dark stillness, near the tremulous edge of the thin veil between life and death, she heard the clarion sound and followed it to this place, to India, like a blind person stepping a sure path on the sound-petals of a loved one's voice. Now, again, she listens for direction like a faithful pup waiting patiently for the voice command of its master.

On this first night of Diwali, her longing to hear the guiding voice intensifies. She is full of hopeful anticipation of this festival to commemorate the restoration of good over evil. But the guiding note does not sound.

Rather, a sad ripple of exhaustion rises and nearly drowns her in a deluge of grief. Sagarika, awash in sorrow, remains by the river all through the days of Diwali. She sits alone, as still as a rock, unnoticed in the happy throng. When the nights of joyous feasting, flower garlands, lighted lanterns, and gift-giving come to an end, Sagarika stands in the water up to her knees and lifts her garments to float on the surface. She clutches two sections of cloth in her fisted hands and rubs them together. She scrubs until her fingers are raw and sore, standing half-bent, scrubbing a stain that will not dissolve, will not disappear. The river will not accept her sin and wash it away. She clutches at her sari, her skin as pale as a frog's belly. She pours a deep loud wailing song into the river's dark flow.

An old woman hears her mournful cries and wades out to Sagarika, puts her arm around the entranced woman and escorts her to the river's edge. She wraps Sagarika in dry cloth and pulls Sagarika's head to her shoulder. The woman's thin, stiff body is strong like steel and holds the weight of the younger woman's body, now limp and heavy with exhaustion, on her own. The old woman gazes at the dark waters and moves her cracked lips in a barely audible tone.

Sagarika awakes alone on a rocky expanse, the morning star hovering on the horizon; a damp chill clings in the air. The outline shapes of curled sleeping backs dot sandy ledges along the river like dark mounds of earth. The stench of cooking, burning, human defecation, animal dung, sweat, toil, and exhaust that permeates every substance has been cleansed by the night and will soon intensify with the heat of the new day's sun. In the quiet hush of pre-dawn, Sagarika stretches her body on the flat rock perch. Two mangos, wrapped in a cloth, lie beside her. This is where she will stay. The river will be her teacher. The river will bring forth a wisdom-song to guide her to the next step on her life's path. She will stay in this place near the river's edge. She will wait.

Chapter Thirteen

Ms. Murti stands at the front of the class. Today she is talking about the elements: earth, water, fire, and air. "Everything in the universe is made of these elements; if we break it down to a rudimentary chemical level, in essence, all things consist of these four elements."

Delia doesn't quite grasp what the art teacher is saying, what this has to do with art. "I want to talk to you about the nature of these elements. First, let's talk about water. What can we say about water? What is water like?"

"It's liquid. It flows."

"Water is clear."

"Uh huh... hopefully."

"It can clean things. You wash with it."

"Water can make itself go into any shape."

"People are made up of a lot of water. They need it or they'll die."

"That's right. Our bodies are made up of about seventy percent water, about the same as the percentage of water to earth on our planet. Now, if we were to say that water represented a feeling, what would that be?"

"Maybe sad… like tears?"

"Or maybe happy—like a fountain."

"Both are true—so perhaps changeable?"

"Yeah, it can be raging fast or kind of mellow and easy… sometimes it just sits in a puddle."

"What are the sounds associated with water?"

"Roaring like Niagara Falls!"

"Gurgling?"

"Splashing! Waves crashing."

"Pelting rain"

"Hissing and bubbling when it boils."

"All these things you say about water are true. Today we are going to explore the element of water in art class. You may work in any color or combination of colors, in any medium, but what I'd like you to do is sit quietly and recall an experience that is somehow associated with water. Then I want you to translate that to the page, or at least try. Get a feeling for water—the flowing, changeable aspect. I'll dim the lights and put on a CD of water sounds."

Delia is stuck like a stagnant pool. She's stuck on a mucky pond bottom. She can't get a feeling for what the others in the class spoke about: flowing, gushing, gurgling, and splashing. She's getting the sensation of a steady drip—a persistent plip, plip, plip—or maybe it's a water drop on a windowpane or beads of snow melting on a woolen coat.

Delia sits slumped in front of a blank canvas and then slowly, imperceptibly at first, it wells and builds in her until it's an onslaught; she wields her brush like she's Poseidon, the great god of the sea, brandishing his trident; she conjures a raging rogue wave that threatens to snatch her by the ankles and topple her over and sweep her away. She paints dark, undulating swirls with ultramarine blue, deep sea green, murky mud brown; her wild wave builds momentum and breaks abruptly, dumping broken-bodied swimmers on a pounded-sand shore.

Delia is the first student to finish the water element painting. She feels content now, as though she's bobbing along on a raft with Huck Finn and old Jim. She feels swimmingly good. The bell/buzzer sounds and she's floated out into the narrow school corridor, bumping and jostling other bodies like flotsam and jetsam at sea. Her feet are touching the floor, the floor of the school, which has a secure foundation upon earth, so the woozy sensation in her gut cannot be seasickness.

She walks woodenly along the hallways and out the door— no hanging around, just out the door. Delia would laugh if she could watch herself and see how she has acquired her dad's manner of walking in lurching strides. Before she's made it to the exit, though, she hears her name.

"Delia!"

She turns to see Ms. Murti.

"Delia, can you meet me in the art room tomorrow after school?"

"I guess so… okay."

Delia fumbles with her key in the front door lock. "Dad?" she calls out to the empty room.

She is curious about where her dad is going off to these days. It's the third time in a couple of weeks that he's not been home when she's arrived after school. There are no lights on, there's no "baked bean delight" simmering on the stove, no "7/11" hello.

Delia wonders if he has a girlfriend or something. It would be okay—maybe he should. He must get lonely sometimes.

She goes to her room and flops on the bed with her iPod. She lifts the back of her legs straight up the wall and flings her head over the side of the mattress as she listens to catch the lyrics of the *Tegan and Sara* track she's recently downloaded:

Throughout believable yesterday
I delayed a stutter that was slowly
Calming me, coaxing me
You're my daydream
Does it make you
Homesick for me?

Delia's dad arrives home and makes a supper of a slew of roasted vegetables smothered in melted cheese and thick slices of buttered bread. A savory aroma permeates the air and drifts down the hallway to tug Delia's senses from sleep. At the edge of her awareness, she knows that her dad stands in the doorway to her room, gazing down on her— her head flung over the side of the bed, her hair strewn to touch the floor. Though her eyes are closed, she can feel him standing there and she knows that the welling tenderness spilling from her upside-down heart and washing over her is washing over him too. In her pretend sleep she sees him take her up in his arms and kiss her on the top of her head; she is his little girl again; everything is different.

"Delia?" he calls with a soft voice to rouse her.

"Delia?" He gently nudges her shoulder.

"What... what?"

"Supper's ready."

Delia and her dad eat in silence. She doesn't feel like speaking. Finally, he says, "Will you pass the butter, dill pickle?"

"Since when did you call me dill pickle?"

"Ooops, I mean pass the dill, butter pickle," he teases.

"Dad, I don't like it!" Delia flings her fork on the table and scrapes the chair legs on the linoleum, thrusting herself away from the table edge. Her dad reaches for the butter dish. He spreads the butter evenly, out to the very edges of his bread slice. He breaks the bread as if performing a ceremonial rite, chewing each piece thoroughly so that Delia can hear his teeth grinding, his throat globbing. She leaves her half-finished plate of soggy-veggie-medley on the table and leaves the room; leaves her dad to eat the remainder of his dinner alone.

"So, what's going on with you?" He speaks loudly so

she can hear him from her room. He's not actually talking to the walls.

"I could ask you the same question," she hollers through her half-opened door.

"Delia... let's talk." He's leaning on the doorframe to her bedroom. He looks at her with quiet exasperation and a hunger to understand.

"So what do you want to talk about?" She glances cursorily at him, as if she's busy, as if she has to leave any moment for an important appointment.

"Us?"

"Okay, so where were you? You always say I should leave you a note and you don't leave one for me."

"Gosh, I'm sorry, Delia. I didn't anticipate being late... but I guess these appointments are running overtime."

"Dad, do you have a girlfriend? Is that it? You can tell me, you know. I'm old enough to handle the truth."

"No, no, that's not it. Just a minute... I have to give you something." Her dad stands awkwardly, scratching at his head, then wipes the palms of his hands on the front of his flannel shirt.

He blurts, "The counselor said I'll know when the time is right for this."

She watches his back, his long, gangly gait; notices the spot on his head made visible by his thinning hair... *counselor?*

A few moments later, he emerges from his room, a large envelope tucked beneath his elbow, and stands before her, shifting his weight from foot to foot, then thrusting the envelope into her hands.

"Delia, I'd like you to have this."

Delia opens the yellow envelope and reaches in to pull out a smaller blue envelope, the color of a robin's egg. She's startled by a quickening sensation at the tips of her fingers that judders her arm and sings its way up the nubbles of her spine. She doesn't remember ever having seen the flowing cursive script, but she recognizes it to be her mother's handwriting.

"When did she send it?"

"She didn't send it. She left it with me a long time ago. She asked me to give it to you when I thought the time was right."

"So, what does it say?"

"I don't know, Delia, it's for you. I'm not sure what it says." Delia holds the envelope—feels its weight— she has no idea what it holds, though her dad's eyes tell her it's important.

She carefully tears at the envelope, as though she's pulling at a loose thread and is wary of pulling too hard and causing an unraveling, "Dad, can I go to my room to read it?"

"Of course."

He goes to the kitchen to make a cup of instant coffee and turns on the radio to listen to the hockey game.

Delia pads off to her room, anxious to consume the letter as if she's about to devour the last chocolate in the box before anyone else learns of its existence.

My dear Delia,

I don't know how old you will be when you read this letter. I owe it to you to explain a few things. First, let me tell you how difficult it is for me to leave. Perhaps these seem like hollow words, but I cannot convey the immensity of pain I feel at leaving you. I have to believe that this is the best thing for everyone. I have broken your father's trust in me and I know that it would be impossible to build it again after all that has happened. I know that your father loves you very much and that you love him. It would be another hurt to inflict on you both if I were to take you with me.

I don't know if you've ever come across the Bible story about two women who claim to be the mother of the same child. They seek the counsel of the wise

King Solomon to settle their dispute. The king says that he will cut the child in two and give a piece to each in order to solve the dilemma. One woman cries out to him not to harm the child. She would rather give the child to the other woman and forsake her claim to motherhood. The wise man knows that this is the true mother—she would rather bear the pain of losing her baby than inflict suffering on it. Can you understand that, Delia?

Yours and Dave's relationship is so special, you are everything to him. I cannot hurt you both a second time by taking you away.

It was all going to be so nice for your birthday and it turned out terribly. I spent a lot of time thinking when I was in the hospital. I just have to shake off all this business with Billy and your dad.

I feel that it's my fault Billy died. He wouldn't have come that day but I called him because it was your birthday and your dad had overlooked that when he booked his hockey team. I was upset with Dave so I called Billy. It's not that I ever would have wanted the accident to happen, for anyone to get hurt, but going out like that, using Billy to get back at your dad, it's kind of poisonous. Somehow, I feel my petty vindictiveness was like the tiny particle that started a wave to form and to swallow us.

Delia, I wish I could take that day back—not your birthday: your birthday is a precious day—but the events of that particular day. The pain of knowing that I somehow played a part in Billy's death and caused the destruction of my marriage is so overwhelming. And I've hurt you too. I feel so bad about what happened. I feel that if I don't make a move right now I will have to lie down and die. Delia, my leaving is me fighting for my life. I'm sorry but I just don't know of any other way to do it. I know you will grow up to be strong and beautiful. You will grow up without me and I have to trust in that—there is nothing else that I can trust right now.

So, my darling daughter, perhaps you can forgive me one day.

I love you always.

Your mom, Cheryl

Delia cannot move. She cannot feel. She cannot cry. There is a black stone stuck in her throat. If she swallows, she will choke. If she doesn't swallow, the back of her head will split open.

Chapter Fourteen

If Delia doesn't pull herself out of bed and go to school, she won't be able to make the meeting with Ms. Murti. She decides to go in midway through the morning. Her eyes are puffy, her lips a little swollen, even though she's submerged her face in a sink of cold water. She doesn't bother to do anything with her hair; she can pull up the hood of her sweatshirt.

It's a Day Two—science, science, phys ed., LUNCH (she goes home and almost decides not to come back), keyboarding, life skills, math. Except for her appointment with Ms. Murti, she shouldn't have bothered.

After school, on her way to the art room, Delia passes by the girls' volleyball team as they're heading into the gym. They're tanned, tall, always talking and laughing. Delia is over her disappointment at not making the first cut on the volleyball team—she wouldn't have liked being part of their group anyhow.

Actually, she doesn't know much about any of the volleyball players except for Brittany Anderson. Truthfully, she doesn't know Brittany that well either— they went to the same playgroup, attended kindergarten together. Brittany apparently doesn't recognize Delia anymore—she had looked straight at her in the hallway just now but didn't acknowledge her existence. Delia slumps her shoulders and glues her gaze to her feet. She lets loose strands of hair fall in her face. She doesn't care if Brittany Anderson ignores her.

She doesn't need friends. Friends would be a complication, an intrusion—they'd want to know how her face got to be this way, and then when they got to know her, they'd want to know what happened to her mother. Delia would play along with their twenty questions, good-naturedly, like a cute little circus person, and then she'd hate herself for being so pathetically needy of their attention. Or else she'd get in with a couple of girls who would use her to make themselves feel superior, tossing subtle put-downs and feigned insecurities her way. "Delia, do you think this looks ugly on me?" or "Delia, my hair looks awful, don't you think?"

And what could she say? "No, you don't look ugly, you don't look stupid—you look gorgeous and you know it. I'm the ugly stupid-looking one."

Anyhow, she likes the relationship she has with her dad and she can always talk with her Aunt Shirley, which is way more interesting than the gaga conversations of girls her own age. She's fed up with people who feel they have to be nice to the poor disfigured girl or who use her like a receptacle bin for their insecurities. She's not going to let anyone do that to her anymore.

Delia waits in the art room, thinking Ms. Murti must have forgotten their appointment. It's twenty minutes after the bell when Ms. Murti enters the room. "Delia, I just spoke with your father on the phone. He tells me you're having a bit of a rough time. Anything I can do?"

"I doubt it."

"Well, let's talk about art then."

"Are you from India, Ms. Murti?"

"I was born in India but I came to Canada when I was a little girl. I've lived in Calgary most of my life."

"My mother was born in Calgary but she went to India when I was a little girl. Don't you think that's kind of weird?"

"No, I don't think it's weird."

"It's strange—I just read a letter from my mom for the first time; she wrote it seven years ago, and in it she says she feels like maybe she was a little particle that got a wave rolling. It's strange because I painted a wave in art class, on the same day I read the letter."

"Perhaps you could say it's synchronistic."

"Synchronistic?"

"A psychologist—his name was Carl Jung—he created that word because he believed that not everything that we *say* is a coincidence *is* a coincidence. He thought that sometimes a coincidence could mean something more; that perhaps it may have to do with something greater, with the alignment of universal forces."

"That sounds weird."

"Maybe it just means that a coincidence is not necessarily by chance, but by design. What do you think—your mother's letter, the wave you painted—a coincidence or something more?"

"I don't know... I'm kind of confused... I've been confused for seven years, actually."

"It sounds like you're struggling."

"I wouldn't say struggling. I'm okay and everything. It's just that everything is so complicated and it doesn't have to be."

"Then why is it?"

"I don't know... that's a good question."

"Well, if it doesn't have to be, then likely it will change. Delia, I notice that you really immerse yourself in art class. You seem to be the kind of person who can work through things with creativity. Art, music, writing: these kinds of things can be invaluable friends."

"You mean like my only friends."

"You'll make friends—when you're ready."

"When I'm ready? It's not that I'm not ready... it's just that other people . . ."

"Other people what?"

"Nothing. It's just that other people wouldn't understand."

Delia takes the long way home. She dodges traffic on Memorial Drive, zigzags through neighborhood streets, and walks along the river path. It's a sunny autumn day. Moms push their kids in carriages; a few people ride bikes or roller blade; old people stroll. One woman—she must be a professional dog walker—leads five dogs on leashes. Delia juts off the paved path and steps her way down the bank to the river's edge. The river runs clear, rippling over smooth stones.

Delia has seen the emerald-colored lake from which the river flows. It's up in the Rocky Mountains west of here. The water comes from glacial melt. Some people say that global warming isn't happening, but if you go up to the icefields near Bow Lake you can practically see the glaciers melting before your eyes. She steps a narrow path through wolf willow and wild rose bushes. The grass that grows tall and green, waving plump seed-heads in summer, lies flat and brown now. A few tufts of silvery withered sage and wild purple aster poke through the grass mat.

Delia rock-hops through shallow water to a large smooth boulder. She pulls her sweatshirt down over her bum and draws her knees up inside to sit on the rock and gaze at the rushing river. Bits and pieces of hollow reeds float on the water's surface. Her eyes follow the course of the floating stems until they're out of sight. When she was little, she'd come here with her mom and dad and they'd drop sticks off the Edworthy Bridge, tossing them on one side, then dashing to the other side to see whose stick emerged first from beneath the bridge span. When you dropped your stick, you gave it to the river; you merely watched to see what happened. There was nothing you could do to affect the course of your stick, nothing you could do to make it move faster or straighter. Delia thinks most of her life has been like that—like she's the flimsy stick abandoned to the rippling current.

A pair of mallard ducks bobs along, their fat little bodies tilting so they're bottoms up, exposing curly tail feathers, paddling their leathery orange feet to keep them steady while they dive for underwater delicacies. Delia admires the ducks; she thinks they are lucky to be so well suited to earth, air, and water. She considers herself to be ill equipped to navigate any of these elements. She feels like an alien.

Chapter Fifteen

"Aunt Shirley, did you ever feel like quitting school?" Delia inserts questions between slurps, a bowl of frosty flakes held to her chin so she doesn't spill milk on the new couch.

"No, not really. I liked school. It was a way to get out of the house."

"Why did you want to get out of the house—I thought you had that whole happy family thing happening."

"Jeez, no. My mom and dad bickered all the time."

"Really? I didn't know that."

"That's because grandpa and grandma mellowed as they got older, and then they moved to Vancouver Island so you only got to see them once in a while, on summer holidays or something when my dad was off fishing. My parents made each other miserable—and that made us miserable." Aunt Shirley sets her clay cup on the glass tabletop, rankled at the sound of glancing contact. She rubs her fingers across the lines on her forehead as if she could smooth them away.

"I always thought you had a wonderful family life."

"That's a laugh. I got along pretty well with your mom, but Sheila and I fought about everything. She used to take off with my new clothes. I waited tables at Nick's Steakhouse all through high school, bought my own shoes, boots, jeans. Then she'd take off with my stuff and disappear. I wanted to kill her."

"I don't believe it. You're always so mushy with her—you always hug and everything. I wish I had a sister to hug."

"Well, you've got me—I'm always up for a hug. Sheila and I—sure, we hug but we don't have much in common. She's been in Vancouver quite a while now. She hangs with the beautiful people, you know, the artsy-fartsy-I'm-so-smartsy types in their hemp clothes and trendy haircuts, carrying around cloth bags from the health food store and smelling like patchouli oil."

"Patchouli oil... what's that?"

"When I was younger we all wore patchouli oil. Some kind of essential oil, from India, I think."

"What's wrong with that? Why don't you like it now?"

"It's not that I don't like it; I just don't like people thinking they're better than other people because they shop at a health food store and recycle their garbage. Most of them don't have any concerns. They live off government grants—they don't have to make the kind of compromises that people who have to work for a living do. Sure, I'd like to ride my bike to work every day and get rid of my car. But I worked a lot of hours at a shitty job to get my wheels—and they're so short-staffed at the restaurant that I've got to be there at a minute's notice. I can't ride my bike when I've got to be there ten minutes ago, can I? Sheila and her friends— they're grinding beans for lattes and reading poetry while I'm starting my shift."

"Aunt Shirley, I thought you liked your job."

"I don't hate it."

"But do you like it?"

"I wouldn't mind doing something else but I'm over thirty now. What am I supposed to do? How can I go back to school and pay all the bills?"

"Would you want to go back to school? I can't wait to get out."

"You think that now. But wait a few years when you've got debts and you're stuck in a crummy job. I was in a hurry to get out of school, too. My girlfriend and I got an apartment in Kensington as soon as we graduated. Then she left and went to university and I stayed on—we'd signed a year's lease. I got a car and had to make payments, pay for gas, insurance, a cell phone, all this stuff." She gestures proudly with a sweep of her arm though Delia hears the crack at the back of her voice.

"So you didn't really plan for things to work out this way, you just sort of fell into your life?"

"You could say that, that I didn't really plan it this way. I would have liked a little house with kids on the way by now. And a man, a man, too," she laughs.

"I thought you said you didn't need a boyfriend."

"I wouldn't mind if a good man stuck around."

"I always thought you were so happy."

"I'm not unhappy. I have a good life, friends, work. I get a few dates."

"But are you happy?"

"I'm not going around with a smile tattooed on my face. I'm mostly okay and sometimes I have a real gas."

"When? When do you have a real gas?"

"When you come over for the weekend or when I go salsa dancing with my friends or when I'm in my car and going down a backcountry road to the mountains. There are lots of things that make me happy. Sometimes I get lonely."

"You get lonely? You always seem so above that."

"No one is above getting lonely."

"Do you think my dad gets lonely?"

"Of course. Everyone does."

"I don't. Except for my mom—I get lonely for my mom all the time."

"Delia, your mom's been gone for more than half your life—and it's becoming more than that each day. What are you going to do? You can't stay lonely for the rest of your life."

"Why can't I? I can if I want to." Delia sets down her bowl of soggy cereal and flops back onto the couch to stare at the ceiling, as though it could reveal something to her.

"If you really want to, I guess you can. But why would you want to?"

"It's not like I want to want to. It's a feeling, I can't help it."

"You know, Delia, sometimes a feeling comes crashing like a bulldozer—but I decide how long the bulldozer stays; it doesn't get an unlimited parking space."

"Do you believe in synchronicity, Aunt Shirley?"

"When a coincidence has some greater significance?

Sometimes. Once my girlfriend and I were driving down
Deerfoot Trail and we were talking about this guy I really liked, making an elaborate plan, contriving a way for
me to meet him and then—we're way down on the other
side of town, down at South Center Mall, and I never go
down there—and he's coming through the exit door as
I'm going in."

"What did you do? Did you talk to him?"

"No, I didn't. I felt too self-conscious and then
I never saw him again. Someone told me he played
university ball but I guess it wasn't at the University
of Calgary. I went to all the games but he was never in
the lineup."

"Do you regret it, regret not talking to him?"

"Yes, Delia, I do." Aunt Shirley rises abruptly to
retrieve a small cylinder from the book shelf. Delia
watches as she removes the cap and drops granules,
one at a time, to the solitary fish that swims in a bowl
at the center of the table, cooing and chirping as
though she were feeding a baby.

Delia leans her back on the edge of the art room sink. There's a chance that Ms. Murti will drop into the room for something. Delia doesn't have an appointment and she's not sure that Ms. Murti hasn't gone home for the day. She surveys the art room walls to look closely at the drawings and paintings. It's obvious to her that someone in the class loves animals—chalk pastels of dogs, cats, turtles, and frogs are done with lots of color and big curvy lines. Someone—someone seemingly obsessed with skateboarding—has done a series of black ink drawings with buildings and stairs and oversized skateboards that appear to be soaring right off the page. Dark charcoal sketches of stark bent trees are strung along the back wall above undulating blue-green swirls and spatters.

Delia finds her own portfolio on a shelf. She opens the cardboard folder and takes out her work, spreading it on the floor to have a good look. She kneels down, touches her fingers to an awful lump of red that is one of her paintings. Another paper is smeared blue as though someone's used it to clean up a spill. Jumbled yellow layers make a kind of collage. Primitive purple figures, like something a toddler would draw—circles and sticks—compose another piece.

"Delia?" Ms. Murti has come into the room without Delia noticing. "What brings you to the art room so late in the day?"

"I thought I'd look at my portfolio... pathetic, eh?"

"No, not at all. I really did mean for the students to explore, to get a feel for color. Most people sought the safety of form; they painted things they knew—cats, dogs, people, trees. There's nothing wrong with that, but you took up the challenge and painted color. I think you've got a feeling for it."

"You do?"

"It seems you're not afraid to let some of your inner feelings be expressed in your artwork."

"I'm not?"

"That's how I see it."

"Maybe. I know I'm not afraid to admit that I'm a freak."

"Let's say… unique."

"So, if we disregard my face, does not knowing whether your mother is dead or alive make a person unique?"

"I imagine it would be hard."

"It is hard—not knowing where she is—whether she's alive even."

"You mentioned before that she was in India." Ms. Murti speaks distractedly as she stands over Delia's painting of a dark wave. Delia doesn't want Ms. Murti examining it so closely—it's messy, ugly.

"My aunt told me that my mom sent a card from India once. India's a big country—I guess you know that—I don't know if she's still there. She could be anywhere. Have you ever read *Who Has Seen the Wind*, Ms. Murti?"

"Yes, I have." She bends closer to observe Delia's painting.

"I was reading how Brian gets this feeling—kind of mysterious and sometimes it hurts. He wants to feel it, not only when he's happy but when his dog dies, when he sees that barefoot boy on the prairie; it may be God or maybe it's realizing you're growing up and you're not a little kid anymore; you see the world differently, the beautiful things, the ugly things—did you ever feel that way, Ms. Murti? Do you think it's weird...?"

"I think it's natural for a person to want to understand about life and death. We get so busy with daily life it seems we're unaware of these things—that a capacity for joy is related to our ability to feel sorrow, that compassion has to do with acceptance of our pain. I think most people have thought about these things—it's not weird."

"Ms. Murti, if my mom is alive and living in India, what would her life be like?"

"I don't know that, Delia. I don't know your mom."

"But if she were living in India, would her life be different?"

"All the choices that any of us make... those things shape us. I took a pottery class once; the man who taught the class had been a potter all his life. The lines in his hands were permanently stained; his skin had absorbed the pigment of clay. The ends of his fingers were wide, like the spade ends of shovels, shaped by running his fingers over clay on the wheel. What he did physically changed him, shaped him. Whatever we do, whatever we choose, it changes us, perhaps not leaving a visible sign as in the case of the old potter, but, yes, I think that we are changed by what we do."

"So, do you think, Ms. Murti, that what a person feels and thinks inside of them shapes them too?"

"I believe that the inner reflects the outer or the outer the inner—something like that," she says distractedly as she puts her hand to her forehead. "Delia, it's late in the day. Let's put your portfolio away. Would you like to display one of your pictures on the wall?"

"Uh… I'm not sure… okay, I'll put up this one." Delia closes her folder and returns it to the shelf. She's left one picture on the floor and she takes it now to the back wall of the classroom. Ms. Murti searches in her desk drawer for thumbtacks and hands them one at a time to Delia.

Her dark whirling wave is up on the wall for anyone to see.

Chapter Sixteen

Delia plunks frozen perogies into a pot of boiling water. She watches the plump, doughy moons dance, suspended in the bubbles. When they've boiled for a bit and softened, she drains them and fries them up in a pan with a little butter and a handful of diced onions. She's already made a Caesar salad, without the anchovies. When Delia's dad wakes up—later than usual—he'll be surprised to smell the good aroma of onions in butter on the stove.

Delia notices that her dad seems tired lately; it seems to be since he gave Delia the letter from her mom. They've not really talked about it; she's not sure whether to initiate a conversation. She can feel her dad stepping near her with caution, skirting softly like she's some motion-activated explosive device or a cracked piece of china that's been glued together and could possibly fall apart at any moment. It's not like him. Usually when there's some discomfort between them, he lets it slide; enough time will pass and whatever it was will go away.

"Smells good. What's the special occasion?" Her dad emerges from his room and glances to the table that's nicely set. There's even a candle stub propped in an old wine bottle.

"You're always doing the cooking. I thought I'd give you a break. Dad, you don't look well—you're tired all the time." Delia lets words jump from her mouth— words that convey what she really feels.

She and her dad sit down at the table as though they are two mature people looking forward to a leisurely dinner hour engaged in authentic conversation.

"Thank you for making supper, Delia." Her dad speaks sincerely before placing his napkin on his lap. He offers a few pleasantries and then asks, "How's school going?"

She would like to tell her dad that everything is fine—

marvelous, actually. She'd like to keep their polite conversation pinging along as though it were a little white ball, back and forth, without dropping it or sending it flying over the table and across the room. Instead, she tells him the truth—how much she's hated school these past few years. How much she's hated her life.

She's incredulous when he replies, "I didn't know that—you seem to be doing well—your report cards are always good."

Delia's impulse is to blurt infuriation, but instead of unleashing a spate of accusations like pebbles and dust spraying from a squealing tire—*you're not paying attention, Dad!—you don't have a clue about what I'm feeling!*—she tells him that she's felt crappy about her life for a long time. He listens, and though he doesn't speak, Delia feels enveloped by his attention. Then she tells him that it's starting to get better, that she really loves her art class. And how, previously, she had avoided art because she was afraid that she'd suck at it, but she's found that she likes painting—expressing her feelings—and not getting hung up about whether her paintings look right. And though she'd expected to hate L.A. class, because usually she's read all the books and finds it heavy-duty boring, she likes that the students are given some choice as to what to read—it's not a force-feeding session of the same old books and the same old multiple-choice quizzes and homework assignments. Delia is aware that her dad is trying hard to listen—he puts down his fork, he looks at her, and his face becomes soft and open; he's not scrunching his forehead as if trying to figure out a correct response before tiring of the effort.

She is amazed when her dad swallows the last doughy morsel of perogy, then clears his throat and shifts in his chair and speaks to her. She is incredulous when he starts to talk about his sessions with the counselor. She leans toward him, as if her physical proximity could attract each one of his words into every cell of her body. She can't believe that he's speaking to her so openly and unguardedly. She's careful not to interrupt or move suddenly; she doesn't want to break the spell, burst the bubble, trip him into clamming up or glossing over with a pathetic attempt at humor.

He tells her how he realizes—through the counseling sessions—that he'd been so mad at Billy. Then one day, he realizes he's mad at Delia's mom, not Billy. He speaks in a low voice, relaying what he'd told the counselor, how he'd rehearsed in his mind—a thousand times— what he'd say when she came back: he'd be angry, detached, disinterested; he'd shut her out; he'd rail about a litany of the things she'd missed in Delia's growing up years. He'd forgive her completely. He had never considered that she wouldn't come back. He'd been expecting a phone call, an e-mail, a knock on the door for the past seven years. He'd spent those years waiting, imagining what he'd do, what he'd say. All the while, he's been careful to do his duty, keep a steady job, make a nice family home for Delia.

She listens attentively to her dad, who sits across the table from her so that his face wavers in the candle's glow. She feels a surge of compassion, feels grateful for all that he's done. It occurs to her that he's left out a few details—such as how he's constructed a nice watertight life so as to try to shield her from the pain of knowing the truth. Such as other people. Even though they sit down to eat together and the house is always presentable, there are never any other faces at the table, there are never anyone else's shoes at the door. Sure, Aunt Shirley drops by and sails into Delia's room for a few minutes every now and then. Once in a while her dad's mom calls from Fort McMurray—she remarried a few years ago and moved with her new husband to start a business up there, a combination laundromat / Internet café. At first she called every Sunday, but she's busy now and she rarely has a minute to get to the phone or to a computer, if you can believe that.

Delia wonders whether her dad notices that she never brings home a friend, that she never talks on the phone. Does he think it's normal for a thirteen-year-old to hole away in a room, appearing only to make blender concoctions of yogurt, banana, and coke? She knows he sometimes speaks to Shirley, concerned that her erratic emotions may have to do with female stuff—she overhears him whisper, "hormones," but he doesn't talk with her about it. He doesn't appear to be aware that Delia keeps people away intentionally; that she uses a mark on her face like a line in the sand over which other people cannot cross. Perhaps, she thinks, she's learned this behavior—keeping other people at a distance to guard hurt—from him.

After supper, they clear the table and do the dishes together. In the middle of drying a plate, Delia's dad drops the towel, sets the plate on the counter. He moves across the floor, so that he stands squarely in front of Delia, looks into her eyes. "Delia, the person I'm really mad at is myself. All these years being bitter, not getting on with my life."

The class discussion today is about the element earth: strong, solid, cold, fertile, life-giving, stable mountains, blowing sand, our planet, our home.

Delia introduces earth to water on her page. She colors with oil pastels, layering and blending the pigments to create satisfying hues. She wants to create a gentle wave rolling to a friendly sand shore, a rocky ledge, nodding sea grass, and delicately bent trees. The picture on the paper is nothing like the picture in Delia's head. Each attempt to right the scene obscures her intent, transforms the scene into something foreign, something not right, like the time she dropped off a roll of film at London Drugs and received someone else's photos; she had looked at them again and again, expecting them to be different, but they did not change. She has created what she can only call a mess on her page. She snatches the paper, crumples it and tosses it into the trash can. She performs this series of events twice more before giving up altogether and slumping in her seat for the remainder of the class. When the room is emptied of other people, Ms. Murti speaks to Delia.

"I notice that you're frustrated. Do you think that's an excuse for not trying?"

"What do you mean? I tried." Delia attempts to conceal a whine.

"Delia, I have the same expectations of you as I do of everyone else in the class. Lots of people have challenges in their lives." Ms. Murti looks at Delia with clear, steady eyes.

"So? *Your meaning?*" Delia's body stiffens as she crosses her arms and lifts her chin to Ms. Murti.

"When I was a young girl, my family lived in a small townhouse—my parents, five children, my uncle, grandmother. We worked, all of us, at a bottle depot, for less than minimum wage. People in the complex where we lived complained to the managers that there were too many of us, they didn't like the smell of our cooking, that we hung our clothes outside to dry. It was hard, very hard, to live in this strange, cold country. Especially hard for my father. He was a respected man in India, but here he worked in a bottle depot and he had only to look forward to becoming a taxi driver. I am not complaining. I am trying to let you know that many people have had to overcome challenges, Delia. You're not the only one."

"I never said I was... I'm not feeling sorry for myself, if that's what you think."

"I don't presume to know how you're feeling. It's been a long day. I need to go."

Delia is stung by her awareness that she'd painted Ms. Murti into a nice picture—there was Ms. Murti, a beautiful young girl, long, thick hair, a strand of bells on her ankle, painting happy scenes of her childhood—exotic animals and swaying trees and buttery-skinned people in brightly colored silken robes. Delia is embarrassed that she had never considered Ms. Murti as having a life outside of being Delia's pretty and talented art teacher.

Chapter Seventeen

Delia sits on the leather couch in her Aunt Shirley's living room, surfing channels. There's nothing on. Shirley has gone to the chiropractor and will be home in a half hour or so. Delia gets up and rummages through Aunt Shirley's DVD collection—nothing she hasn't seen. She paces restlessly and then heads to the kitchen where she drapes her arm on the open refrigerator door, leaning inside to survey the contents—nothing much here, either. She opens a jar and fishes out the one fat pickle soaking in brine, munching it while she leans on the open door and peruses the possibilities for snacking.

She wanders through Aunt Shirley's apartment, goes into the bathroom, opens the cabinet door. There are a few old prescription containers, a bottle of pink stomach stuff, a can of hairspray, six shades of nail polish, dental floss, tweezers, band-aids, a "Joy" perfume set still in the box, nail polish remover, hand lotion, a razor with blades, and up on the left top shelf that's coated with an oily layer of dust, a gold ring. Delia picks up the ring and examines it closely. She notices an inscription on the inside of the band and tilts it toward the light fixture to make out the tiny letters: *Shirley & Tom 01/22/98*. Delia's heart races as she slips the ring on her finger.

She hears the door close and the sound of Aunt Shirley taking off her boots and hanging her coat in the closet. Delia flushes the toilet, turns on the faucet for a minute, and emerges to greet Shirley.

"So, kiddo, I see the place is still standing. What do you want to do for supper... feel like Chinese?"

"Sure... Aunt Shirley, can I ask you something?"

Shirley eases onto the couch. "My back feels a lot better; I could barely move yesterday. Fire away," she says.

"Is this a wedding ring?"

"Someone's been snooping... yes, it's a wedding ring."

"How come you have it?"

"I have it because it's mine. I was married for six or seven months."

"What happened?" Delia stands in the middle of the room, her mouth hanging open.

"I thought things were going along fine... one day I come home and he's gone... he'd been having an affair with another woman all along."

"That sucks."

"Well, it used to suck, but I don't even think about it anymore. It's like a chapter in a very thick book. I barely remember the details."

Delia speaks in a careful, thoughtful tone as she sits on the couch near Shirley. "How come you never told me?"

"I didn't know you'd be interested." Shirley puts her feet up on the black lacquered coffee table and crosses her ankles.

"No one tells me anything. All this stuff happens and no one tells me."

"What's more important is the here and now. Chinese or pizza?"

Delia has finished reading *Who Has Seen the Wind*. She feels a bit sad to put the book down, to be done with it. The students in L.A. class have clustered in three groups for novel discussion. Brittany Anderson is in Delia's group. Delia is only vaguely aware that Brittany has been in the class all along. Now her chair is next to Brittany's in the group at the back corner of the room.

Delia is sure that Brittany Anderson will pretend she doesn't know her. Delia is prepared to do the same. But then Brittany leans over and whispers, "How's it going?"

"Okay."

"It's been a long time since I've seen you—since kindergarten, I guess."

Like I only see you in the hallway all the time, thinks Delia, derisively.

"So what's new?"

What's new? How considerate of you to ask. Delia lowers her eyes, making her face neutral to conceal disdain, "Not so much. You?"

Brittany cups her hand over her mouth and speaks in a hushed tone. "We moved back to Calgary a few months ago."

"I saw you on the volleyball team—how's that going?" Delia wants to let Brittany know that she received Brittany's snub.

"I had to quit. I don't have time for it."

I'm sure you have way too many terribly important things to do.

"My dad rolled his tractor; he's in a care facility. My mom and I moved back here so we can be closer to him."

"Oh... I'm sorry about that."

"It was pretty bad, but it's getting better. My mom's got a new job, so that's good... but now she doesn't have much time to visit him, so I try to get there most days... Your mom, how's your mom? My mom was talking about her the other day... wondering...?"

Someone is asking me a question about my mom. Someone was wondering about my mom. I'm a person just like anyone else with a past, present, and future.

Delia has been brought face to face with the very thing she's been struggling to avoid. It's like a story she read as a child, where the boy is terrified by a monstrous thing that looms in the dark, and the thing turns out to be fed by fear—the more it's feared, the larger it grows. When the boy is able to befriend the monster, it shrinks to become a tiny thing.

"My mom's doing pretty well, I think... I think she's living in India now."

"Oh. That's cool."

"Yeah, sort of..."

"Class, we should be discussing the novel. Choose one person to begin and then go around the circle. Let's be sure everyone gets a chance to contribute with no interruptions. Let's say three minutes per person and then a five-minute wrap-up with the whole class at the end. Any questions?"

Delia sits in the circle; she listens and observes other students as they discuss the book. There's a guy who's overweight, hair plastered on his forehead, glasses.

Another guy wears a shirt with a collar, his hair neatly trimmed, his basketball shoes whiter than white. A tall girl wearing high-heeled boots that go up past her knees smoothes her hand over her hair while incessantly bouncing one foot. A girl with dyed black hair has a piercing on her eyebrow and one under her lip. Two girls wear T-shirts and designer jeans; they both have colored braces on their teeth and wear "Run for the Cure" bracelets. Brittany Anderson dangles her crossed ankles in the chair next to Delia. She wears a light lime-green shirt, black pants, and flat, soft leather shoes; she joins the discussion only once, but her contribution is thoughtful—she speaks with confidence.

Delia sees the other students as if she's washed her eyes with water from a fairytale's magic crystal fountain. She sees them as if it's the first time. She sees—clearly sees—them: thoughtful, assertive, smart, sexy, cool, self-assured, capable, bad-assed. She sees them: scared, confused, insecure, not-good-enough, how-do-I-look, who-should-I-be, little kids.

Beyond the heads of the people on the far side of the circle, Delia sees Mrs. Arbuckle intensely engaged in a discussion with another group of students. Her expression is serious. Her stiff hair is like a sail, moving when she does. Her head tilts slightly as she looks out over the rim of her glasses. Delia chuckles to herself; Mrs. Arbuckle is not so bad after all.

Beyond Mrs. Arbuckle, on the other side of the windows, is a small grove of aspen trees, slender limbs bent, leaves trembling in the wind. Beyond the trees are streets and houses, and beyond these runs the river; having threaded its way through mountains, it courses through the city's center, beneath highway overpasses, past glass towers, through Chinatown, and on past the place where the two rivers meet. On the eastern edge of the city, the river becomes wider; the water slips along like silk, rippling through rolling grassland. All sorts of creatures are drawn to the flowing water: pelicans, swallows, ducks, beavers, coyotes, deer, and people.

Delia thinks about next June, when she and her dad will set off in a canoe from McKinnon's Flats. She will not fret about whether to paddle left or right, to pull or pry. At some point along the journey, she will draw up her paddle and lay it down. She will sit back, surrender to the water and let the current carry them along. She is sure that she will be able to do this because, here and now, her feet are planted firmly on the ground.